All big cities have organized crime, drug kingpins, and hit men. Nevertheless, every now and then the police find out through someone in the organization not being able to hold their tongue or the police have infiltrated the organization.

Two teens Indio and Pryce are exceptions to this rule, they both have been planning this for three years in separate corners of the city, Indio in middle class neighborhood and Pryce in the projects. Only Pryce looks to have his cake and eat too. Pryce has made it out the Ghetto and now living in a middle class neighborhood. When Indio and Pryce team up who share the same vision, the diagnosis is kaos for the city and those who cross their paths.

For 12 years, they have committed more murders than the mob and more crimes of theft and armed robbery than all the mafia organizations in the city. No one suspects the teens from this middle class neighborhood are capable of this level violence; none of the local gangs pays them any attention they do not register on the law enforcement radar. During school hours, they are A, B students, athletes in football baseball and basketball, chores around the house, working for New York City summer youth employment program part-time jobs that keeps them low key. On the weekends and holidays they are party animals, in between they make more money than the Federal Reserve can print. All are planning to attend college, military, the political power they obtained comes not from rubbing elbows with politicians because of their status but the people in their organization are senator's congressional representative, mayors and council members. To add to this resume of the East New York dynasty, are judge, prosecutor and top criminal defense attorney in the city, security consultants, financial advisors, Ceo's and Business owners.

Nobody knows these men, are part of the most deadly organized crime syndicate in the City, but when three men seek to reveal the identity of these men and expose them for what they have done. One man decides to give up his entire career to protect his brothers, he goes to prison, Philly and South Carolina to hunt down the ones who seek to destroy their dynasty. After killing Anthony Brown on the city streets the rest, go in hiding.

Despite her dislike for Brown, his murder hit home and she wants to know why. Dolly is the top organized crime prosecutor for the city, and her boss has just handed her the file for action on the East New York dynasty. The folder on her desk has one piece of paper that reveals the names of the snitches and she quickly alerts the dynasty, the death of a prosecutor brought heat on the mob. Anthony was not only investigating the East New York dynasty but the Italians, Cubans and Koreans, Antony killing was the copycat of one of their well-known hit men and this allowed Christopher Marinelli from the Federal Prosecutors office to arrest all the top bosses of each of the five families.

When Jessie "Marble Eye" Santiago kills Dolly boss mistakenly every law enforcement agency has placed him on the most wanted listed of NYPD and Federal agencies, but the dynasty knows that if the police reach him before they do it could be over for them. They find Jessie in South Carolina prison the last thing he saw was the man he met years ago but no idea that he was going to kill him, now the man who risked his entire career for them now must make it out to clear his name. However, the only person who can help him is missing, and the Prosecutors office is on high alert with two dead and one missing. The dynasty and Dolly family are out looking for her, the dynasty know who it is

Chapter One:

Red Hook

Red Hook, Red Hook what good memories I leave you Red Hook

My mother took us from you to a place brand new

Leave us lamenting. Now we can only guess

What reason can we use our empty hearts?

No will not be coming back here anymore

Some day our tears will end, but oh, we know!

When we went riding on that highway

Now old friends would turn out to be new.

We will have to start over, with all new white faces.

Can you make young kids hesitate, to make the change?

Chapter Two: Lost Innocence

The Fourth of July was supposed to be a good time for scarecrow, Booboo gave him some firecrackers to sell and he had already sold 30$ of fireworks for him and still had more to go. Out of that he was going to get $10 which for is age was a lot of money, he had plans on what he was going to spend it on and on his way back to his house he ran into Jeff.

"Hey scarecrow Anthony wants to buy some fireworks from you"

"Okay lets go" unaware of the danger that lurks in Anthony house scarecrow is escorted by Jeff Antony cousin to his house. While they walk, Jeff conscious eats at him for what he is about to do, and in his mind he rather do this than have anyone find out he is gay. Scarecrow asks Jeff how much Anthony wants.

"All you got"

"Listen I must go to the house and get the rest, all I got now is four packs of firecrackers and two bottle rockets."

"No just give him what you got and come back later with the rest"

"No when I sell these I will get paid and will be finished with this, so wait I will go inside to get them" despite Jeff insistence scarecrow still goes inside to get the rest of the fireworks and when he comes back out they go to Anthony house.

16 Mill Street is adjacent to 31-center mall and when they enter the building, no one is suspicious of scarecrow going into the building or into Anthony house, which nobody saw them do. After they enter the house, for some unexplained reason scarecrow feels uneasy but only wants to sell the fireworks and get the hell out of this apartment.

"Come in and have a seat you want something to drink"

"No look I just want to sell you these fireworks and go so how much do you want? "

"Ok I thought you might want to stay a while and talk, we'll just have a drink while I go get you the money for the rockets and firecrackers."

"Ok "he goes into the kitchen and fixes scarecrow something to drink, and gives it to Jeff to bring it to him. After drinking what appeared to be kool-aid and despite him just sipping the drink, he begins to have a real uneasy feeling inside, the lightheadedness has him so dizzy that all he could do was sit down on the couch. The last thing he remembers was Jeff giving him the drink, but when he began coming to his senses he realized that Anthony was on top of him,

"Hey what are you doing, get off me "

"Stop moving you know you like it"

"No get off me please get up I-I-I" all he could do was cry at the thought of this man violating him in the cruelest way and no one to help. However, the one person that could was in the closet watching the entire thing go down, and he was the reason he was in the house in the first place.

"You like it"

No stop or I will Kill you" all Anthony does at the remark is just laugh

"Well that's good just say you like it and I will stop" through the tears scarecrow says what he does not want to say

"I like it please stop your hurting me, please it hurts please" the pleas to stop only allowed him to continue and this caused scarecrow to black out and when it was over, he awoke got dressed and ran out the house not worrying about the fireworks or the money he just lost because of this. After he blacked out, Jeff left and Anthony put money in his short pants pocket. He had no idea scarecrow had awaken, while he was on the phone with his other predators talking about what he had just did to scarecrow and how good he looks, and what scarecrow did not hear was the conversation about the picture he took of him naked and would show when they came later in the week.

What scarecrow experienced is what most of our young male and female teenagers living not in suburban neighborhoods but the urban neighborhoods where violence is the social norm, poverty, dropouts, drug addiction, alcoholism, teen pregnancies, and grandma-raising kids is even with death rate in these urban neighborhoods.

This male is fighting to get out, and know that some make it out, others have died trying to get out and others never make it out this sexual abuse war zone. A child fighting for what all children in these urban neighborhoods do best, is fight for their survival in a never-ending battle that continues from one generation to the next, and avoid becoming casualties of this urban war zone.

Presented against the background of Red hook projects in Brooklyn New York, is about project living conditions and the heartbreaking struggle to visualize one-self in these surroundings. These social, economic, pressures create frustration, disappointments, and hostilities among this kid. . Now he is experimenting with cigarettes and drinking, the pain is not over because each day the predator is coming to the house and playing his family into believing that he comes to see them but the reality is that he is trying to get close to scarecrow who wants to be nowhere near him. This kid embodies the hopes, dreams, failures, and frustrations, of the children in an emotional and economically depressed society where the American dream is lost to him. Apparently he thinks the kid was kidding that he wants to kill him, but if someone gets to him before he does then good but scarecrow is seeking the death of him if but for no other reason but for what he did to him and the pain that he has caused him will be hard to overlook or disregard. The question is how and why has he picked him and what he did to deserve this, which set him up and how, many other kids has he did this too. These and other questions will have to wait now, but the future will hold some answers that will surprise him.

This kid is typical, incapable of giving up about anything he knows that what happen to him should not have happened. He has a sense of pursuit of life, but whether it is still alive remains a mystery. Sexual abuse has made many young teens stray from there course that god has set for them and scarecrow is no exception. Despite his belief in God, he has not as most do curse god for what has happened to him but he closed himself within his own world. The feelings of hopelessness have not even set in, because of the abuse and to some he is still the same person. His predator looks at him like he was a turkey on thanksgiving, only he has all ready carved him up and now scarecrow wants to carve him up. He is adamant and persistent in coming to his house, he has his parents believing he is a nice person but scarecrow knows that he is not. During his time such things in black neighborhoods was never talked about and to accuse an adult of such things will bring the wrath of the parents, nor would a grown person believe this and so now scarecrow and countless other children are left to deal with sexual abuse. Who do they turn too most drugs, crime, homosexuality and some overcome it; now the only question is which road will scarecrow go. Will he become a junkie, criminal or gay it is too early to tell but scarecrow is determined not to become either one just the one who overcomes this. This kid has waged war on his predator, to ensure that his dreams are not lost to the abuse he has suffered because of this. This child need for love, dignity, achievement, and continuity makes him relevant to children outside New York's Red Hook Projects and presents a realistic anecdote for change and for the personal troubles of this child and our communities.

Chapter Three:

"She Did It for Love"

In 1977, at age eleven. Eddie Gulstons a childhood friend a brother from another mother. In Red Hook, everyone knew we would stick up for each other more than we would our own siblings. In that same winter, mother had just graduated from school and participated in a march on City Hall in New York City to get better playing jobs for blacks. All the grownups who took part in this march came back, and decided it was time to leave the projects and they did not bother discussing it with us. We stood around listening to this conversation and recognized our ironclad bond was about to break. These grownups told us to go outside and play, but we did so grudgingly. Ms. Virginia was Eddie mother and our mother's best friend in the projects, who whenever my mother or his mother would go out they would be together they had a bond like us.

Ms. Virginia asked, "What is wrong with you two?"

Eddie answered for the both of us "You grownups need to thaw out because the -10 degree weather has frozen your brains" and she had a better backhand than John McEnroe did because when she slapped him and I caught the back draft.

Before they could say or do anything else, we grabbed our coats and ran towards the door. While sitting on the stoop, trying to figure out why he said what he did so I asked him.

"What! this is pay back from the last time I got us a butt whipping" his lack of retort and the scorn he has on his face made me realize that it was just that. While sitting on the stoop and asked at the sometime.

"When we leave how we will stay in touch"

Made a pact that whoever leaves first had to come back and let the other know his new address and phone number. We decide to walk, and walking through the projects became a final tour, bringing back good and bad memories of our childhood in Red Hook, of games played in Coffee Park, old factories no longer open, looking out over the water watching the tugboat slowly creep past us making waves as it passes. The same waves this boat made which splashed against the docks, is the same as what our parents did when they made the decision to leave.

How inconsiderate it is of our parents, to take us out from a place of peace, security, and people we have grown to trust. No place could ever give me or provide me the type of solace Red Hook has given me over my childhood years what could possibly be better than the projects.

This might one day be just an old memory of a good childhood, just as these docks was once the center of trading for these factories, my childhood is on the verge of becoming like these docks.

Eddie had tears in his eyes, which I assumed came from the minus 10degree cold wind that was blowing or could it be that my friend was showing that soft side nobody else knew about but us. It would not be the first time he showed emotion while we were together, although it might be the last cannot help but wonder why he is really crying. Nevertheless, the silence is broken when he asks.

"You not cold scarecrow "I realize my coat in my hand.

"No" was the reply not the way this move has us feeling now anyway, why are you crying? He said!"

"This might very well be our last time standing on this dock, or our last time walking through our hood my friend."

As always, Jeffrey interrupts Eddie classical bonding moment, and that we normally have with one another. Jeffrey walked up before we started crying real tears. Hey! Scarecrow, Gumby Knew this where you two were at. What brings you two to the boon docks?

Eddie explained to him what our parents were planning, attempts to put on a good front; we know deep down inside the news has hurt him.

"Hey look it's too cold to stand around, let's go to the park and play football."

Playing football was only a temporary relief, because when the game ended we returned right back where we were.

Three games of football on a ground as hard as the concrete around it, frozen from bitter but typical New York winter. The games are over, and we head home unfazed by numerous gang tackles and the fact I was made to block a kid who was the size of Fat Albert in one game or being sacked by same kid twice in second game until I decided to run or get the hell away from him.

Stopping by Jeff house for hot apple pie and butter pecan ice cream, talking about the game only allowed us all a chance of reflection on something other than moving. Night has fallen and streetlights are on so Jeff sister takes us home, she is our pass for being out after streetlights have come on in our hood is the curfew. Make it safely inside with no repercussions, to me and Eddie 5:30pm is early but we go take a bath, just to beat our 8pm bedtime gives us one hour. Heading straight to the tub already filled with water quickly undresses and get in and begin washing and once finished drying off. Heading towards bedroom to put on pajamas, and while in my room Eddie busts in "You slow "no Eddie I washed but somebody in this room did not! We both know who that is! We both laugh and that is when he says our parents have gathered. So ask where and he says

"In your living room"

As we head out the room all our siblings are waiting for us, our family was fond of calling us Frick and Frack or Courageous Cat and Minute Mouse. We sit down and our parents tell us what we both already know, that we were about to move and the only thing that we did not know was where. Since nobody has asked the question of why, I did, and while not expecting an answer everyone looked as if what I did was something terribly wrong.

Nevertheless, at such a young age the response was the equivalent of not answering because it made no sense. Mother said living in projects is a stepping-stone to build oneself up not to continue living in poverty when you can do better. Now it was Eddie's turn:

"So why not continue living in the projects to save money to buy and live well in the projects?"

The simple adult answer is that we are not moving for us, but for you to have a better life and while it is hard for you to understand at present time always know we are doing it because we love you.

Respect of life and limb kept any further comments that

"If this is love hate me" Did not come out.

In addition, but everything we heard was not comforting to either one of us. Later while in the bedroom, we talk about conversation that did nothing but add to our dilemma.

On Sunday morning for the first time, mother begins reading Daily News Real Estate Section and notice she has areas marked off all in Brooklyn, really made no difference since had no idea where these areas were.

Grandmother is ready for church and so are older brother and sister, it is just luck, today is the junior choir anniversary, and we have to perform after church. Really wish it could be cancelled, so that I can plot on sabotaging this move and as a good Christian, I finally decide on putting it in god's hands, because perhaps he has a greater plan for me in this move and just too young and just perhaps when I get older it will be clear. Oh! Nevertheless, who knows one day could be making same type of decision, but at the present must trust that "She did it for love."

Chapter Four:

Training to Kill

New York winter is typical at 7:30am at 25 degrees as the weatherman reported. Inside the Smith and Johnson households, the air is warm with the love one would expect from families living within the projects which is nothing more than the city prison for its downtrodden or lower income recipients or the poor. Today is Monday and breakfast with his friend scarecrow every Monday morning is common for the families and. Therefore, when Gumby knocks at the door scarecrow mother and other siblings know it is no one else but Gumby. When scarecrow sister and brother says

"You two are ridiculous just one day will you two be alone?"

"We already did that, this summer with me going to the fresh air fund for two months and looking to go back"

What good did it do you wrote to each other every week."

Look that is my other brother"

Mommy only had three boys not four, his brother says as Gumby walks in the door well she don't know it but this is her long lost son and I found him"

So what am I?"

You really want me to answer that question"

Yes! His brother says and so would I scarecrow mom says

"Chopped wood to be discarded when needed not before, everyone laughs even Gumby

I guess my family was talking about me, just like our family scarecrow always trying to figure us out. The comment was in reference to the ironclad bond of these two, but what no one else not even his friend knows that scarecrow is training with his boss Mr. Kim in the martial arts, military tactics.

His mother leaves a list of chores for them to do and scarecrow quickly reminds his mother that he has to work after school. Once Gumby and scarecrow finish eating they are the last ones to finish eating so they clean the breakfast dishes before\heading out the door.

The walk to school is a short distance from the projects, and it takes them no time to get to the school. P.S.27 is the public school for the projects as well as I.S.142, separated from the hood by an overpass that goes over the Brooklyn battery tunnel, the school is filling up with kids from the hood and the school bully tiny approaches scarecrow and Gumby. This is no normal kid he is far taller than others are and has the strength of a man that has been wrestling with cows all his life, and when he comes too Gumby and scarecrow he is unaware that scarecrow is now ready for battle.

"Ok you two what did I tell you?"

Gumby is the first to respond, "We forgot remind us again"

I told you that you are not allowed in the school yard until the gym doors open, so now walk back out the gate and wait"

Now scarecrow turn, "well sorry we are already here and I have no intentions of leaving so"

"I never asked you what you wanted to do you are going to do exactly as I say or else"

"Tiny the only thing I fear right now is the bad odor coming out your mouth, now stop breathing on me"

With that, Gumby quickly grabs his friend and begins to move away, but the other kids who heard the comment by scarecrow are still laughing and that only infuriates Tiny even more. He begins walking quickly behind scarecrow and Gumby, but scarecrow senses his presence and continues with the remarks.

"I guess you have no idea what a toothbrush and toothpaste are, welfare money buys those things try it for once"

Tiny was so enraged by the skinny kid who he has beaten up numerous times now has the heart to talk to him like that, as he hurls back to swing on scarecrow saw him coming moves out the way only to allow Gumby to get hit with tiny fist. As Gumby falls back scarecrow moves in quickly and the moves the kids saw can and could only be done in Hollywood but this was not Hollywood this was the pjs and the fight was not what tiny expect neither did the other kids.

Nevertheless, when they saw how scarecrow handled Tiny, it was the talk of the school even the teachers who witnessed the fight called the principle. Who stood and watched as the skinny kid beat tiny like he was his child, when the teachers protested that it was enough and scarecrow did not, which is when the principle came to pull scarecrow off Tiny. Mr. Diamond grabbed scarecrow, as if he was a piece of paper and took him to his office. Once in his office he called scarecrow mother and told her what happen, but she explained to the principal that she just started her new job and could not leave. She told the principal to call her brother, which he did and when scarecrow heard him call his uncle Bootsy name, he relaxed. He loved his other uncles but Allen and Gary only gave lectures that scarecrow did not want to hear especially when he was the one getting his ass kicked all the time. His uncle asked to speak with scarecrow.

"Hello"

Boy what happen it's not even 9o'clock and you fighting already"

"It was not my fault I tried to leave the but Tiny would not let me leave"

At the sound of Tiny's name, his uncle and the principal already knew that the bully got whatever it is scarecrow did to him his uncle asks

"Did you win or get your ass kicked again"

"I won"

"A lie don't care who tell it as long as it's told"

Scarecrow picked on in the hood, despite the constant fights he had, he was still not the skilled fighter one would expect from the hood and always ended with the lost. However, the principal heard the question over the phone.

"It's no lie he beat Tiny like he was the parent and tiny was the child"

All his uncle could do was whistle, I will be there in twenty minutes to pick you up and take you home.

"Hey unc you think you can take me to work, no need sitting round the house.

The wait in the office was calm and the principal talked about the way he beat Tiny, and they both laughed at that. The principal told scarecrow that he was sending him home and to return in the morning

"We'll say you got sick and had to leave Tiny will have to come up with a good lie about the lumps he took today," they are both laughing when his uncle walks in the door.

"I miss something?" he asks

"No just the fight and beating"

When his uncle looks at him, he sees no scars or bruises on him.

"I thought you were fighting?"

"He was only his opponent never had a chance" the principal responds.

His uncle has a bewildered look on his face, but he is still shocked at what he is hearing. Could it be that now his nephew has started to get better at fighting, or was he just lucky today. The only person who could answer the question was scarecrow and he was not telling anyone about his martial arts training and Tiny nor anyone else in the hood stands a chance, his bony chest is sticking out very far and the fact the girls are looking at him differently gives him more pep in his step. Even the teachers are cuing in on the scene, see you tomorrow slugger get some rest.

As they exit the school, scarecrow loves riding in his uncle deuce and a quarter, the car is sitting out front with his uncle right hand man, and scarecrow adopted Uncle Willie. These two are just like him and Gumby friends from the childhood and now crime partners, only he is not involved in anything illegal yet.

Uncle Bootsy is the hustler of the family, his bankroll is just as big as his harem of women and with that comes many children. The last count was 12 children 7boys and 5 girls, that is why he is still in the game to pay for all the children he has, the ride is fun he got the chance to finish talking to his two uncles about his plans.

"So my two favorite uncles tell little nephew how do you have an organization, that nobody knows about doing the same thing the mob is doing but only better"?

"How many people do you plan on having in this group?" Willie asks

"Oh about 12 and an elite security team that only I know about"

"Sounds exclusive but there are flaws in the plan"

"Like what unc?"

"First, you need to find the people for this, second, how are you going to keep people from knowing who you boys are?"

"Well the plan is to make sure that during the day we go to school, and at night we spring into action and during off days of school. Each time we meet or do anything, we will wear ski masks.

'Sounds like you got it together, so how are you going to assemble the security team you're talking about?"

"Well that is why I have you two hustlers, to help me get it together"

"Really, well I guess we have been recruited. So are we a part of the gang?"

"No you too old, I need your wisdom and assistance nothing more will you two help me when the time comes?"

"Yes" both says to him

"But you need to get the security in place now, remember one thing if security is slack then your life on the streets will be short. Take me for instance I have been your uncle security for years, so you need to find one person you can trust with your life and recruit him on the team."

This sounded good but scarecrow does not know if he could trust Gumby, it has been four months since Anthony molested scarecrow and scarecrow has not told anyone of this not even his two uncles. During his training with Mr. Kim, said that the only way this could happen is if someone real close to him allowed this to happen, but the thought of Gumby allowing this to happen was something scarecrow did not want to believe. Mr. Kim told him that you could not move on to the next chapter of your life if you keep reading the same chapter again, to scarecrow after further explanation from his teacher he was told that the demons that haunt him must be killed or they will kill him.

They pull up to Vanderbilt apartments in Brooklyn on Newkirk ave in Flatbush, and go inside the apartment which is nicely furnished three bedroom apartment one for him and the other two for his women and him. He sees his uncle dump a bag of what he called baby powder on to the table and he asks them.

"Why are you two pouring baby powder on the table?"

"Look sit in the bedroom for a minute" Scarecrow goes towards the bedroom, only to see two people having sex and he peeps. At first glance, scarecrow thought it was a man and woman, but when they turned, he saw two women getting it in and the way the other had her head between the legs of the other girl. The sounds of life made it clear she was enjoying it, the two see scarecrow and call him into the room.

"Look instead of watching, come join us" the short black petite woman gets up and grabs him by the hand.

Scarecrow is nervous but he is a willing participant, as the two bring him to the bed they take his clothes off and begin playing with his Johnson and watched it erect. He jumps on the bed next to the one who took him by the hand, and he lays back.

"He acts like he knows what to do Margie; you know how to eat pussy"

"What is that some type of new food, but willing to try anything with you two except for the baby powder they have on table out there."

The two women laugh at the comment by scarecrow, but they give him the experience most men dream. Too have sex with two women at the same time, they stand over scarecrow with their pussy in his face and show him how to eat, as he begins Margie begins to moan Oh yes Th—at the spot oh yes lick it like It's a lollipop

"I'm trying to see how many licks it takes to get to the center" scarecrow says as he begins licking between Margie's legs as if he was eating A Strawberry Shortcake ice cream and all those in the room enjoyed the ride even if he was underage. The entire time his uncles were looking at him, with the two dikes he sleeps with and pays the bills. They went looking for him after they finished bagging the heroine, only to hear the sounds of life coming out the room and peeped in door and saw him lying nude while the two had his nephew eating them as if it was not his first time.

The sex was good but it was time to go, when he came out the room all his uncles could do was smile at him. Nevertheless, he paid them no attention and went into the kitchen to get something to drink.

"Hey unc you know I love you, but your nephew is too young to drink beer so why do you not keep kool-aid in the house."

"I only have to worry about that when the other nephews and nieces come over not you, because you have no problem popping the top of a beer can or bottle.

All the men laugh at the comment from Uncle Willie.

As they get set to take scarecrow to his job, his uncles grab their guns and he wonders why they did not have them when they came to get him.

"The gun is like your arm you would never leave home without so why did you two leave yours?"

"Willie responds, who told you that?"

"I got it from the both of you"

On his way to Fifth Avenue where he works takes longer, his uncles had to make stops that allowed him to see firsthand what his uncles are doing. As they get out the car in Busch wick section of Brooklyn on Quincy ave, the bar looks as if it is ready to be condemned but inside the tables and floor plan are immaculate with a long bar hugging the rear wall and the live band playing music rehearsing.. Instead of following directions from his uncles, he comes into the office with them, and sits in the back while they sit in front of the office desk. The owner of the bar Mr. Gavin is an old time player from the cotton club days a tall muscular build person about the same age as his uncles, one person on his right is his bodyguard watching everyone except for scarecrow. Scarecrow places his Dan Wesson 38 with 9" barrel and silencer attached in his lap, the man thought it was Phony.

"Why you brought your nephew and I see he got his toy gun, young man taking lessons from your uncles they are the best in the game you will learn a lot form them?'

"Ok now that we have that out of the way, let's get down to business"

The whole time Uncle Willie face does not reveal that his nephew has stopped playing with toy guns years ago and if he does have one, it is real. His only question," how serious is his nephew about using the gun?" hope we do not have to find out in this room, it will be hard explaining why he was with them. The family has no idea that scarecrow goes with them all the time, but this is the first time they see him with a gun. Complements of Mr. Kim his boss, which is training him to use guns and build bombs, and use his hands to kill any man that he fights.

During the conversation with his uncles, the man tone is changing and getting more irate as the conversation continues, but Bootsy is also getting and matching the man tone.

"Look we are not here to negotiate or discuss this; it is going down the way I say and nothing less will be accepted by me or my partner."

"Listen your nephew is present, so let's not get trigger happy with him in the room."

"Trigger happy I see nobody pulling out guns, or are you planning to do so" Willie says to Mr. Gavin

"No but you never know, accidents happen" with that the room got deftly quiet and it even made scarecrow nervous and before his uncle could tell him to leave.

At the mention of being trigger happy scarecrow fires one shot into the bodyguards' chest and he falls. Scarecrow gets up and walks to the desk.

"Look my time is limited I have a job to be at in an hour so do as my uncles are telling you."

Willie is looking at his nephew with the gun in his hand and any doubt erased from his mind of how serious he is about killing people. His nephew just got his first registered kill or is it, and knows there is no turning back now.

"You been training him to kill I see" the man behind the desk says

" No not me, but yes he has been training, now if you would like to see the next hour do as my nephew asks you to do or he will add you to his body count"

"Ok we have a deal but only if he is controlling the operation"

"No do not trust you, besides why should I trust you after killing your bodyguard?"

"You not afraid of me are you little boy?"

With that scarecrow fires one shot in the man head and he slumps over in the chair, he takes the gun and tucks it back under his coat. Nobody heard the shots with the silencer.

"You two ready to go, and explain what operation I will be running". Scarecrow is the first out the door, and his uncles follow him. The bartender does not bother to look at them, when scarecrow goes to the bar and tells him that the place is under new management all the man does is laugh. Nevertheless, the look on scarecrow face, the man quickly stops laughing and looks at the two new owners' well three owners, the kid is young but the ice-cold tone of his voice and facial expression makes it easy for bartender to take him serious. The bartender has been around long enough to know a killer when he sees one and the bartender knows either he has killed before, or set for his first kill and the bartender wanted to avoid being one of his first or many victims.

As they walk out the door, with his two uncles behind him he walks out as if he was the don and his uncles are his henchmen. Uncle Willie gets in the back and Scarecrow is in the front, but before the car pulls off a barrage of questions comes too him from his uncles. "Yo where you get that gun from?"

"You already know the answer to that, so now the other question the answer is the same why ask something you already know about" Scarecrow says matter of factly

"We had no idea of this but, look next time give us a heads up"

"Well my two favorite uncles, you need to be more on point the bodyguard was reaching for his gun that's why I shot him and for his boss smart remark I killed him. Bedsides he was planning to kill me if I ran the operation"

They both agreed with him, and realized that scarecrow has really been listening to everything they have talked about in his presence. The ride was long but it still allowed scarecrow to arrive at work at 12 not the normal time but Mr. Kim will be glad to have him. Scarecrow does not know that August is out of school for the same thing, and they both will be in the store working. They told him that the operation is selling heroin and that he has now taken over Bed-sty area heroin market now.

His uncles told him they would run it until he turns 15 which will be in three years, and that suits him just fine it also gives him enough time to get his plan into motion. As he tells his uncles, "Look out world a new player is on the block"

Uncle Willie pats him on the shoulder and they laugh as they listen to Otis Redding on the 8track tape, they arrive at his job and Mr. Kim and August is out front talking. When they see scarecrow, it is a surprise but both see something different about scarecrow one that Mr. Kim recognize

"Why are you not in school?"

"He beat up the school bully," his uncle tells Mr. Kim

"It seems like these two both have been doing the same thing, well I have him now I will have him fed and home by 7pm"

"This suits his two uncle's fine; they are still feeling the effects of the double homicide compliments of their nephew. Not only was he responsible for the murder of their competition but he was also, the reason they got connec in Chinatown. While they go back to the car August and scarecrow are already at work without mixing words, and Mr. Kim is getting ready to spray water on the fresh fruits and vegetables Ms.Kim comes out and tell, her husband.

"I think scarecrow has just killed someone, he has the look you had when you first killed"

All Mr. Kim could do was look unfazed by the comment and dismiss his wife as hallucinating, and try to assure her that scarecrow is not ready for such things.

"Do you doubt him or your ability to train, because it seems he has passed the test?"

Mr. Kim goes back to watering the veggies and fruits, but in his mind, he wants to see if his wife is just hallucinating. So tonight he will put his two sons to the test, he will give them a contract to kill someone but only it will not be easy to kill these people without a gunfight he is only hoping they are the ones to walk away. If not he will be burying two of his own not paying respects to the ones he had killed, but that time world only reveal the readiness of his sons goes without saying.

The day is over and the store is getting ready to close as usual at 5pm, August is sweeping and Scarecrow is restocking the shelves and coolers for the next day. While Mr. Kim gets ready to close the register, two white male come in the store and point a gun at Mr. Kim

"Yo chinks give me the fucking money"

"Please not now" Scarecrow says aloud

"Look nigger shut your mouth"

"I hate that word"

I said shut your mouth"

As the other robber with gun approaches Scarecrow, he puts the gun away and approaches him.

"Now be a nice nigger and be quiet"

"Stop calling me that, cracker"

"Oh we have a live one well let's see how lively he is when I beat his little nigger ass"

"Please if you do not know what your doing do not mess with him"

Mr. Kim tells them but he knows they will not believe him, so when he sees they are insisting he lets it all go down. When the person in front of scarecrow mashes him in the face, scarecrow does not budge only his head move the body stood firm. The man gets indignant

"Oh tough guy"

"Please quit while you're ahead, the life you two save will be your own"

In his mind he still wonders why people think that someone as small as him is easy prey, well that was before Mr. Kim now after him nothing is easy. The predators will have better luck with Moses, than they will with him. After four(4) years of training under Mr. Kim and continuing the young kid is a trained killer, with a weapon or without these two guys are about to get something they do not want or expect.

"So you think you can handle me little boy, well let's see how good you are"

The person goes into his stance, but scarecrow is standing his ground and has not moved. The only thing that has move is the boxes of Ajax that he is placing on the shelves. As he gets up and looks the man square in the eyes, looking for signs of an eminent strike that soon came. The man made his move, only to truly regret his move and his partner called himself following his partner who was three times the size of scarecrow when he tried to join the fight. What they thought was the skinny kid would not be able to handle two big people at one time, but they miscalculated and after seeing his partner like a flat tire he hall butt out the store so fast all Mr. Kim could feel is the breeze of him passing him.

The fight was over before it got started, and scarecrow is looking at his teacher who nods his head with approval at the way he handled himself. The other storeowner who saw what took place called police but scarecrow is still from the hood and he wants no part of the police and goes in the back with August and his mom. The police have one of them perps in custody and the other hauled butt after he saw what scarecrow did to his friend, the other is sure to tell because his friend looks as if he cannot hold water.

One the other Korean storeowner came into the shop, he offers to take scarecrow home but Mr. Kim tells him to take his wife home. Because they have some work to do, it will be scarecrow next test. Mr. Kim is not counting this one but so far so good for teacher and student, even August smiles along with mom how scarecrow beat the snot out of the robber partner. What neither of them know is that the Genovese crime family is responsible for the robbery that has taken place, they want Mr. Kim to pay for protection and he refuses and that is the reason for tonight's visit to send a message. A deadly message, before this gets out of hand and his two sons find out what the mafia is trying to do to him and he knows that the results could prove fatal for the mob and the city. The mob hates everyone outside of their race and a black and chink will only infuriate the mob more, and create havoc in the city with an all out war on the streets.

After the drama from the botched robbery, Mr. Kim made a call and within thirty minutes two cars pulled up in front of the store and four big Koreans got out the car and walk into the store. These men at first glance look normal but the call scarecrow knows made by either Mr. Ms. Kim , brought these men and the first too exit the car scarecrow knows him from the training he put him through these past four years. This was not a social visit, not after what took place in store and scarecrow and August know that those responsible will have hell to pay for this. They are also aware the mob has been putting pressure on their father to pay for protection, but Mr. Kim told them in so many words that the only people he will pay is his own personal security.

The boys heard his father and mother talking about it one day, and both think the mob was behind this robbery today.

"I sure like to find out if the mob had something to do with this" August tells scarecrow

"Yeah so would I, to put a bullet in the head of the man that allowed this to happen" Scarecrow tone was serious and it made August ask the question that has bothered him all day

"Hey have you killed someone before" the question-shocked scarecrow so much the look on his face told the entire story.

"Listen promise me you will not tell none not even your father or mother" when he said it August was all ears for what he was about to hear, but his mother was also listening to the conversation of these two

"Ok I promise no one will know" Scarecrow looks at him for any signs of doubt, but as always there is no doubt, he could trust him with this.

"Yes I shot a man today in a club for my uncles, the man was pulling out and they were so into the conversation they paid no attention to the bodyguard that was pulling out on them."

"How did you get away without anyone seeing you?"

"My gun had a silencer on it and besides who would think a little boy pulled the trigger on a kingpin of the hood"

Scarecrow told August about his fight in school and the killing, and when he finished it was as if scarecrow had lifted a burden off his shoulders. He had a good ear from August, as well as his mother who he had no idea listened to what they were talking about with a smile on her face. As she turns to leave the door, her husband and soldier slash bodyguard, run into her and ask what she is doing.

"All I will say is they are ready for the next level" the bodyguard is confused about what she is talking about but Mr. Kim is not, only he still finds it hard to believe they are ready so soon. As she head towards back door she turns and says

"I was right he did kill someone, and it was today" this shocked him to the point that it took the bodyguard 15 minutes too snap him out of the trance. When he comes to his senses, he calls for August and scarecrow, they come out of their office that none enter but them. Which mother and father respect, is the hiding place for the guns and ammunition they have stored. The guns range from six 44mags, 4 38's, 12 44 auto-mags with silencers for all his guns, 9 380's, 2 shotguns, sig Sauer automatic, and 1 grenade launcher. The grenade launcher and M16 came from the bodyguard as a gift for passing the gun course, they know how to clean, reassemble and disassemble every gun in the room.

Kim told the boys they were going with him, to go and get ready and meet him outside in two minutes. As the two head to their office, they are trying to figure out where they are going. One thing was for sure that no matter what, they were not going anywhere without steel on their side and copper in their pockets. When they get in the office August goes to his dresser and pulls out the top drawer, which contained all his 45's al kinds from different manufacturers, he chose the two pearl handles, goes in the closet, and grabs a bag of 45ammo. Scarecrow has a military chest given to him by the sane bodyguard, and when he opens it his 38' are on top and underneath are 357mags, but scarecrow chose his two 380's and fitted silencers on the guns, while August was standing at the closet grabbing his ammo he ask him to give him the small nylon green bag. This bag contained all the ammo scarecrow needed for the ride, but for some reason he thinks this is going to get ugly and great minds think alike because August revealed what scarecrow had been thinking.

"You think we need more than this, I have a feeling this is going to get ugly"

"We on the same page, so let's bring Kaos and baseball to help out just in case"

August shakes his head in agreement, at the suggestion. He knows who Kaos and baseball are and if they have to bring them out then they intend to count bodies, and that the only time to bring them out was to start a war they intend on finishing. Both boys beat their father out the door and instead of waiting inside the car they are outside, it is 6:30pm and the thermostat on the side of the bank reads 15 degrees but for tonight, the cold air has not bothered them in the least. The pedestrians walking by notice the boys are wearing nothing more than a sheepskin vest with a thermal hoodie under it, not realizing the armor they have under these clothes one person asks what others did not

"Aren't you boys cold" and keeps walking and all they did was smile at the old lady who looks like she was real head turner in her days but as time went on the facial features was enough to make the devil turn his head. Perhaps from too much sex or drugs but whatever it was, she just needed to say no because it destroyed her entire life. Mr. Kim and his secret police come out the store, and while one of the men close the gates they get in the car with August and scarecrow in the back and Mr. Kim in the front with his bodyguard. As they drive off, Kim turns and tell them that, they are not to get out the car. However, the look on their faces already let him know that this was not going to happen and he did not continue the conversation, just let it go even the comment the driver made did not faze them.

"It's your funeral, so young"

"So you two doubt us or yourselves, which it is "August asks. No comment came from the two men in front and while the ride would be long, it gave the boys a time to get some rest and that they did. However, scarecrow is not thinking about the kills today, which for most would saturate their thoughts but he is drifting off to sleep with the thoughts of what the future will hold for him. When they get to the place of the Genovese family, it is an Italian restaurant with tables for people to enjoy eating when the weather permits, and on the inside, the place gives you the feeling you could eat here forever. When they stop one of the two cars, which had four men in each one is the first to exit and stop in front of the restaurant. The other opts to Double Park in front of the store, which told scarecrow he was in for a long night but for most new Yorkers, this is typical New York behavior. What most of those who saw these cars did not know was that this was not their normal behavior, and the men did not come for a social visit it was going to be a blood bath in this restaurant. However, tonight the main menu special would be linguini with dead bodies, a tip afterwards was not possible.

One of the men open the door and two guards are in front and two in back, while August and scarecrow trail behind the last two guards into the restaurant. Scarecrow sees the punk who tried to rob the store earlier and pulls off his ski mask, and walks straight to him and Mr. Kim sees the same thing and is right on his heels.

"Hello remember me" the young man looks at scarecrow as if he was trash and he was the collector and this pissed him off.

"Look you was not supposed to see my face, those that do not live long after so I said get up and will not ask anymore" the men sitting at the table behind say something that they should not have said allowing scarecrow to unleash his fury on the restaurant with his brother."You must think I am the herb you're looking for," Pryce says well guess what at that Manzullo responds

"No nigger comes and tells my nephew what to do"

Scarecrow does not respond just gives him a cold stare, scarecrow turns towards the table celebrating and calculates how many bullets it would take to kill the entire table. When scarecrow turns around and pulls out the two 380's and begins firing, as he kills each he says nigger, nigger and when he gets to the last man one of the guns click revealing Its empty but the other is not so he says

"Oops niggers please and fires" and looks at the one he told to get up.

"I suggest you listen to the man," August tells him. Nevertheless, the man continues to look at the man in front of him. Therefore, scarecrow reloads fresh clips in the gun, and fires one into the man arm and this time he moves but his life is still over. The bullets in the gun have poison all over them, and when it begins to take effect the man will have boils and sores all over his body, then nosebleeds, vomiting before death even the people at the table would be dead in a matter of minutes if not for the headshots scarecrow took.

All Mr. Kim and the other bodyguards could do was smile, and before scarecrow could continue his killing spree, Mr. Kim asks Mr. Manzullo if his little plot at robbing his store was over, but the mafia bosses are always trying to show toughness in the face of danger and he was no different. When Mr. Kim asked Mr.Mazullo a question, Mr. Manzullo was better off answering. Because August killed everyone at the tables in center aisle and if it was not for his father and scarecrow he would have continued. It was Mr. Kim turn now to speak.

"Are we going to have any more problems, or should I let them continue?"

"Fuck you chinks and the nigger," Manzullo said

"No fuck you "with that August and scarecrow took the Uzi' from the bodyguards and when the clips finished so was the restaurant and waiters. They reload as they walk out, and when they opened the door two cars are coming to a screeching stop, the two guards out front took aim at the cars but behind them August and scarecrow see more men coming down the street

"Get My father in the car now," August yells as him and scarecrow began firing at the men coming, one of the guards are shot by the men in the car. Scarecrow goes over to him and takes one in the leg; his adrenaline was pumping so fast he did not feel the bullet hit and others watched this kid move as if he was a professional moving under the line of fire as they teach in the military. Kim and his bodyguard sat looking at August and scarecrow work together, in getting everyone to the cars and getting out without any serious casualties. Inside the car, August reaches in and grabs Kaos, while Scarecrow grabs Baseball all hell breaks out when they release their power on the people. The ones in car did not stand a chance, and this brought time for them to escape but best thing is none dead on their side. However, two were injured and one had some explaining to do with mom and it was not August.

Inside the car, after calming down August and Scarecrow notice blood on scarecrow pants and he begins to feel the pain of the shot.

“Dad he’s been shot, we need to see a doctor” but scarecrow is acting and talking like nothing is wrong and this brought more joy to his trainer slash bodyguard his boss and August.

“We need to call your mother”

‘No hells no” scarecrow protest “call my uncles at this number. August finished wrapping a towel around his leg and over his protestations both bodyguard and boss told him to allow August to wrap his leg, They took him to one of their doctors, a hospital was out the question they have to report gunshot wounds and with all those dead in that restaurant they would put two and two together. They are far away from the ruckus, and Mr. Kim stops at a pay phone and calls his uncles who are more understanding. They said they would meet them at the address in an hour, he hangs up and returns to the car they are just forty minutes outside of their destination.

Once they get to the address, they quickly open the door and try to help him out but the kid is showing more toughness than they imagined. Scarecrow is walking and while he is hops to the door, he is still not showing any signs this shot is bothering him. After about three hours in the doctor’s office, the bullet removed by doctor and given pain pills and told to rest. Everyone in the room knew scarecrow was not going to do that, even the guard who added fuel to the fire.

“If you believe he will sit down for that long then all of you are crazy now hang out with me while you’re getting better.”

Kim and the other know that these two together will lead to nothing more than death and destruction, further training on the course used by police and FBI agents around the world to deal with hostile environments such as the one they were in tonight. Despite them handling themselves well, they all agreed more training was necessary for him and August wanted to be a part of this, and his father agreed after seeing them tonight. It did not take long for Kim to say they were proud of the way they handled themselves, and the conversation interrupted by the presence of his uncles entering the office.

"How is he?" Willie asks

"Only a bruise, if you let him tell it. But the bullet was removed"

"What the hell happen?" after the comment his uncle just said never mind "Anyway how are we going to explain this to your mother?"

"The store was robbed tonight and one of the robbers shot me" each looked at one another for something better than what he said.

"He has a point the store was robbed tonight and he once again beat his man"

"I see your training paid off; I never knew just how much you'd learn from them. At time you gave the impression you was not interested and paid no attention and most of all you knew everything" his uncle Bootsy says

"All of you really thought that about me?"

Yes, they all said together

"Well sike made you think made you blink, now don't it stink" they all even the doctor laughs at his remarks.

One of the guards tells his uncles to bring him to this address for the next three weeks, which he writes on a piece of paper and gives to him.

Chapter Five:

Contract Killers

It has been almost a month since scarecrow shootout; Thanksgiving Holiday was good to spend with family and friends especially the guard who was injured. Even though he never gave a name, though both August and scarecrow have asked all he would say is that, is my name is body snatcher strange name for the streets. Nevertheless, people in the streets are strange creatures, so why not have a name like body snatcher as long as he does not snatch my body scarecrow thought to himself who cares. One thing they did find out was that he lost his entire family to the Italian mob, killed his family and burned his business to the ground. Before he could retaliate, his old friend recruited him into service to get revenge and tonight was the chance of a lifetime for a man who lost his world this was a sweet victory. His uncles always told him that when it comes to family, they would be his weakness and easier to control because of family. Despite the pain, he felt in his heart, he saw no way in his heart that he could just disregard someone killing them or his family and not feeling any emotion. Life as a killer was getting better, he had three contracts to fill before Christmas and he felt the best way to enjoy the holidays was to get an early start on the contracts and body snatcher was his driver until he was old enough to drive on his own. They are sitting in August room talking about the holidays, and the work they have to do before Christmas holiday. For the first time they are about to work together, because as they were told the situation will be difficult with guards around him twenty-four hours a day. Any attempt will bring the entire neighborhood, no matter how many grenades they bring it would still be suicide, if they were to get in a firefight with these men. Long way from home and in enemy territory that you are not familiar with is a death wish.

They are on Southern State Parkway heading to Massapequa, is a quiet neighborhood that for some reason will not believe the level of death they are about to witness. August and Scarecrow are assigned to kill one of the most notorious leaders, of a china gang that has gotten out of control. The constant disregard for rules has warranted a contract for his death, with 12 attempts has made him more defiant Won Li is a trained Tae Kwon Do expert. Kim has assured the families that he has two that can get the job done, they have already viewed the set up and both have figured on how to reach and kill them without anyone knowing.

The Intel was accurate and as always Won and his guards were out front enjoying the night air, why anyone would want to be out in 15* degree weather is confusing to the boys but the thought disappears when they realize they are out just like them only they will be able to go inside once this is over. Once they kill the mark, they can go inside where the weather is warm and food is good but this is no easy task because this group is well prepared and numerous attempts have tightened security. Body drives the car around the corner to let them out; when they exit the car, both move quickly through the night. The streetlight is in the middle of the street, which only provides enough light that they could blend in with the darkness as they move through yards. Only thing they were not aware of perhaps the Intel missed this little piece of evidence, was the dog that began barking at the scent of the two killers lurking in the dark. Luck was on their side when a cat stopped in front of them due to the dog barking. August threw the cat in the direction of dog, and really got the dog going wild and with everyone looking at the cat not the Negro Gatos, lurking in the bushes with a 380 with silencer pointed at them and August watching the ones on the porch. The music was loud enough to muffle the sounds of the silencer, under the window the music was coming from nobody knew the two kids were firing at Won Li and his guards all dead now, and before the ones on the porch could react August kills them instantly..

Mission accomplished, nobody saw them leave as they turn the corner and get in the car. Scarecrow watches one man come out and walk in the direction of the carnage, he will be shocked to see that someone has finally accomplished what nobody else has been able to do. Scarecrow does not intend to allow him to get that far, so before he could reach the carnage he releases two shots in his head as they walk by him. Not only did the man not see this coming, but also nobody heard the shots and the way scarecrow has the man sitting it looks as if he is just sitting down.

"Let's celebrate, your choice of restaurant," the body snatcher says to them

"Let's go to Kim's restaurant," Scarecrow tells him. This means they will be going to china town where the restaurant is located, and it also means that when they see them alive it means one of two things either they completed the task or backed out of the job. All those who know them, will surely tell anyone these two will not back down from the devil so the idea of them abandoning the kill is not in Mr. Kim mind. What these two have no idea about is that if they complete this task, Kim status and his family given the recognition it deserves.

The ride to the restaurant is long but pleasant, but the future that he slowly begins to detect is materializing before his very eyes. Besides his two uncles have been noticing a slight change in their nephew, but it was nothing to be alarmed about because he still acted like he could not fight and when the other kid saw that is was not what they wanted they always came to the house and complained about scarecrow starting fights. Nobody believes this because everyone knew; people were always picking on him. When he fought back which was rare, nobody gave it much thought about who started fight. Only thing that puzzled his uncle is why his nephew, who knew how to fight would just lose intentionally, let some of the kids beat him. Even after Willie and Bootsy found out, they thought at first glance it was crazy but what he said to them now makes since. People think that because you lose one fight, you cannot fight, and if you win, everyone will think you got lucky so they will keep coming whether you win or lose. Nevertheless, as he told them the big bullies of the hood he demolishes them but the others he lets them win.

Once they reach the restaurant, and get out Mr. Kim and the other China Town families are inside the restaurant eating. When they see the boys come in, Kim excuses himself at the table and goes over to the boys who are unaware that they knew Won Li was dead and the Dragons were declaring war on the families.

"So let's go finish them off," August suggest. Body dismisses the thought, and tells him that the only way to end this war is too hit them in the heart.

"So where is the heart and how do we reach it, besides I thought he was the heart?

"No the heart was inside the house".

"So we have to go back and kill the house?"

"No not the entire house but just a few people that have a substantial amount of influence over others"

Kim tells them for now enjoy the moment but the others must go, at your leisure time and besides the families are pleased with the results.

As Kim leaves the table and returns to his, the families do not even think the kids he was talking with are the ones who killed the thorn in their sides for the past two years. August, Scarecrow and Body are enjoying their meal and trying to get scarecrow to eat some seaweed by virtue of Its name knows it does not sound good or will it taste good, after some pressure he tries the food and to his surprise he likes it and eats more than they do.

"I was wrong for once what other kind of Korean food should I be eating?"

You really want to know?" the way the question was asked all scarecrow could do was say never mind and go back to eating his seaweed which he had to admit was good. On a typical Saturday night, he would normally be home with Gumby watching T.V., but as time progressed, his weekends were anything but normal anymore. So now, his 6hours of early morning training with lessons in SWAT team tactics. Kids his age were supposed to have fun at his, but he was to be a killer and he had no idea why he chose him of all kids. What happen to him was not his fault but what will happen to the person that did it to him his death will be his fault for what he did to him and countless other kids maybe in the hood or outside the hood but his death will relieve the community of this predator.

Chapter 6:
New Kid on the Block

School starts in September, the first day of school for Pryce in I.S.88 and a long way away from the local schools in Red Hook projects. As he enters school not knowing anyone, it makes him nervous and the white boy watching him does not make things better. Scarecrow still remembers how the white boys would chase them on Court Street to the safe zone or the boundary line the whites drew for the coloreds as they called it "The Colored Boundary Line". However, Pryce does not know Indio is not white but Spanish.

The school bell rings all the kids are heading inside but, scarecrow is waiting and the white boy is walking with him. Scarecrow has no experience dealing with white people, in his hood he never had to deal with them and when he did, it was only when they were chasing them form out of their neighborhood or theirs.

As the Spanish person strikes up conversation, "You said your name was what

Never gave you my name nor do I want to know yours" Pryce says this with the type of voice that comes from a cold blooded killer, or a mob boss who has no time for small talk. But this does not phase Indio in the least he has been looking for someone different outside the hood too help organize his new gang that he has been planning for two years, but has not found the right people until he saw Pryce. Great minds think alike because while they have not officially talked these two are about to find out that they have a lot in common and that they are going to be the best of friends. The reality is that Pryce has been thinking of what it would be like if he was to start a young mob organization that controls, not just neighborhoods but beyond the extension of New York. Of all the people it had to be someone from another country that neither knows of the pain that resides deep down inside this young black kid from the projects, and his struggles to overcome the abuse he has suffered as a child.

Some would say that is why he has become a hired gun for the Korean mob, to cover the pain by taking others lives as well.

The bell just rang in the school and the kids are heading to their classes, as they enter the homeroom class it is ironic that the same kid he just tried to brush off is in his homeroom class. As much as he tries to avoid him, he knows that somehow this person is relentless and will find a way to strike up a conversation with him. Therefore, instead of hiding he sits next to him in the back row of the class, Indio stares at him with a quizzical glare and just puts a smile on his face.

Hey no hard feelings earlier my friends call me scarecrow, Pryce says as he extends his hand to him.

None taken my friends call me Indio, he says with strong emphasis so what is your real name

My name is Frankie Santiago and mines are Darrel Smith they both laugh. None of this meant anything, when the teacher called out their names they knew each was hiding its identity. Deep inside each one knew that whatever secrets they were hiding would eventually be revealed to each other in due time..

The bell has just rung for them to change classes and since they are in a majority of the classes together, they move together as if it they have no fear, only this brings on hatred from people he does not know and cares not to know. The victory lies in the one who is calmer during battle at least Mr. Kim told him as much when he was training.

As they enter the first class, two male teens and females watch the black kid who just came in the door with Indio. As they move closer to their seats one of them stands up, as he stands in Pryce way and looks him up and down Pryce says well what you posing for animal crackers or GQ magazine. "You got a smart mouth for someone who only weighs 90 pounds soak and wet" Says Spanish teen that looks like he is the star athlete for the school football team.

"Look I am not looking for any beef b please leave me alone, I am not herb you been looking for"

Pryce say this with a tone that made the person tense as it sent chills down his spine to hear Pryce speak. Pryce had no idea who he was talking with, but really, it did not matter to Pryce who this man was he was violating his international air space. Because he was not the only one in the class that felt the chill of his voice as he spoke, the other teens as well as his partner tensed at the spoken words.

The class has begun, and as the teacher Ms. Almond begins she is in her thirties and looking good for someone who has three kids and been married once to the same man, Pryce learns quickly that the kids have a song for the teacher that sounds just like the commercial for the candy bar almond joy. Even though the class is going on Indio, cannot help but notice that Manny is staring at Pryce but his partner is not. This makes Indio uneasy he knows that Manny will not hesitate to kill him, but he for some strange feels that his partner is more dangerous than meets the eye and would soon find out why his friend is so dam calm.

The bell rings it is time for lunch, but Pryce and Indio do not have time for lunch. Is Indio planning to kill him or is this a test to see if Pryce will fight. Pryce grew up in the projects where they fight for recreation and then be friends later. But he was no longer in the projects but an entire world far from the projects that he grew to love, and he was about to be tested as Manny and his friends head towards him and Indio

Yo be on point they coming Indio tells him

As Pryce turns around, he sees just what Indio is talking about, Pryce puts down his Hawaiian punch drink and faces the oncoming traffic and as they stop in front of the Indio speaks before Pryce could say a word

Yo, b what up Indio Says?

Yo this not yo beef ya heard we got beef with Negro not you, says one of the guys with Manny

No b if you got beef with negro you got beef with me so what it going to be, the seriousness of Indio voice made Pryce ease a little knowing that he was not alone and that he would not be the only one with lumps if these guys decided to jump him and Indio.

Manny speaks up "so me and your partner going to fight one on one right now, he needs to know in this hood and nobody speaks to me the way he did."

"First time for everything, because no one ever stood in my way and lived to tell about it, guess we call it a mutual understanding or mass murder"

Pryce says with such cold indignation, Manny face turned red because he was being insulted in the most gangster way that he wanted to kill the nigger not just beat him to death and call it a hate crime.

You got a real smart mouth, let us see if you can back it up Manny says

"Are you sure you want this?"

Before Pryce could finish, Manny swings and barely connects, Pryce was a little slow in moving out the way. But when he recovers Manny was better off calling it a mutual understanding because the beating he took would not sit well with him or those he was associated with, while Pryce did not escape without bruises what Manny had was far worse than what he had.

Indio and Pryce go to nurse office, but the bloody nose and few bruises on his face nothing serious that he could not live with. As they are walking out the office a bunch of kids are hanging around the office and see them come out and Indio tells him in a low tone

"Yo b you just do not know what you did for your status in this school by doing what you did" Indio tells him

"What are you talking about? It was just a fight that is all how much status can you get from a fight we have them all the time in the projects." Pryce says with not a care in the world.

"no look friend it matters when the guy you beat is the second in command for the Hardy Boys one of the biggest gangs in the area, and you not only beat him you brutalized him."

Now Pryce is shocked at what he hears, are you serious Indio

"Yes! Now this is not over, believe that they are coming for us now he cannot allow this to happen and in fact he is about to lose rank if he does not redeem himself" "well man your battle stations partner," Pryce says to Indio

"Already at the station the question is are you at yours" Indio tell him matter of factly

"I am now thanks to you". Pryce says, "Now let's get out of this building and go some place safe to talk"

The ride on the B12 bus was pretty quick since the stops the bus makes are limited as the morning rush is over they head to Indio house for safety and at the bus stop they find out real interesting things about each other.

While Indio has the plan to get it going what he did not have was the wherewithal, the other details like on how to keep their identities hidden was the only thing that Indio had not figured out but Pryce did.

Who would ever think that a bunch of kids were running East New York Dynasty, well this name was not born yet but Indio and Pryce had without revealing it to each other had the same name for the crew.

Pryce was worried about how they were going to screen the men they needed or how they was going to select them, Indio told his friend that he already had a few good men in mind and they would meet them later after school lets out, but first they had to get inside before the truant van started lurking.

The city uses police during the day to prevent kids from skipping school.

Pryce notices that Indio apartment is one of New York most infamous storefront apartments that have the store under the apartment. They walk upstairs and go inside, the door that is slightly open only to find a woman that looks like she belongs on cover girl commercial that he is struck by her beauty so much that he cannot stop staring at her the woman walks by and tells him "Your too young and a virgin"

Well your wrong about being a virgin, I eat pussy better than any dike

"He had a fight with Manny of the Hardy boys' Indio says she stops cold and looks at him

"Ok well if you look like that what does he look like?"

You do not want to know

Hey, can I ask a question since everyone seems to think I am going to die, Pryce says

"What is it she asks?"

"Can I get some before I die I don't want to die a virgin?"

Indio starts laughing and so does his sister, "you two laughing but I'm serious"

No but on a serious note please take the fact that you beat Manny is more of a problem than you think"

Your brother has told me this in so many words'

"Ok! Now what about the crew how are you going to start this if your friend is in trouble with the hardy boys?"

"We have it all figured out and when we do figure it out we will let you know" Indio says as he looks at his sister and friend Pryce aka Scarecrow.

His sister has a look of fear on her face as her brother who wants to start a crew has no idea on how to deal with the problems they are facing now. Indio sister gets up and goes in the bedroom but as she leaves out she tells them "look I am going to make some calls and when I come back you two mob bosses need to figure out how to deal with the Hardy Boys" she leaves the living room and Indio and Pryce go into the kitchen.

While they are in the kitchen Indio pulls out some eggs and sausages for them to cook and Pryce grabs some plates out of the cabinet.

Indio watches him make his way around the kitchen as if he lives in the house, Indio has no objection, Pryce is putting plates on the table and Indio says,

"Oh by the way, family does not have sex with family, so my sister and your sister are off limits to the crew especially mines when it comes to you"

Hey all in the family, besides it not incest only losing virginity" Pryce says and they both smile at the joke.

Indio is putting the eggs that he just finished cooking on a plate, and begins working on the sausage as they talk about their next move.

"So what do you suggest we do Pryce?" Indio asks

"Look in the morning we will go to them and talk and see if we can settle the problem without any more physical altercations" Pryce tone was serious but Pryce can see that his friend has reservations about that. "What is wrong you have the look of someone who feels this is not that type of party?"

'yeah they do not negotiate, look the Hardy Boys are one the biggest crews on this side of the Atlantic and Conduit"

Pryce understood that the Atlantic did not mean the ocean but the street that separates them, and the Atlantic is the same street that the school they attend is adjacent with and is a main connector to other areas of the city like Queens.

Indio continues and Pryce now understands that this is not going to end until someone is dead or Manny wins the next fight something that Pryce does not intend to do unless he does so fair and square. Taking a dive is not in Pryce repertoire, so the question when will the madness end and will he have to show the hood that the new kid is not who they want to piss off.

The conversation continues as they eat the eggs and sausage and Pryce goes in the fridge and grabs some orange juice out of the fridge, and two cups that are sitting on the sink he gives one to his friend and he takes the other as they finish off the food his sister walks back into the room

"Well have you two figured it out yet?" and at this moment Pryce speaks up

"your brother explained to me that my plan to just talk to settle the problem is not going to work so, it leaves us no other choice but to meet them head on in anything they bring our way" Pryce voice convinced Indio sister that her brothers friend was more dangerous than his 90 pound frame let them believe.

"Ok, so you agree with your partner Indio?" his sister asks

"With no hesitation"

Ok then you two is about to see what it really takes to be mob bosses"

One question, I get the feeling that I am not the only one you have told about our plan, so now the question is what role do you play in all of this?"

Let's just say that we are the assassins' that every mob boss will wish they had."

You said we I only see you, how many assassins?

16 assassins whose identity only the three of us will know and they are on their way now"

Ok! Pryce says he looks at her with lust in his eyes and she responds quickly

"Look I am gay"

So!" Pryce says," you can turn me out and still be gay, but on serious note people. As they are talking the doorbell rings and his sister goes to answer it "So our guest have arrived"

Indio and Pryce finish their food as the women come up the stairs and Pryce is surprised, he was not looking for women but men and not only are these women fine as wine but they make Pryce nature rise at the thought of these female killers. Since the kitchen was too small to hold the meeting, they go into the living room to begin talking about their plans and the pending crisis when it comes to the Hardy Boys.

The way I plan this is that since we are so young no one will expect us, so it will be mandatory for the members to obtain their education. During the hours of 8am to 3pm, we will be in school and those who violate this rule, and that is the job of the assassins to ensure our members are in school.

One of the females speak up," So we are babysitters and how long is this supposed to go on"

Indio answers" until we graduate Jr.High school which will not be long for all but three of us.

Then what the same female ask, but Pryce interrupts

Wait, first introductions are necessary, my name is scarecrow and we will go around the room.

Well scarecrow, my name is Joan; this is Marisol, Vanessa, Francesca, Debbie, Maria, Helen, Annie, Jackie, Yolanda, Marlene, Sandy. In addition, you already met Leslie Indio sister.

Therefore, who leads this group, and who wants to take my virginity?

"Look, its 13 of us and we are all gay, and you far too young to handle all this pussy

"You wanna try me and find out" Pryce tone took them all by surprise and this made Marisol respond

Ok after the meeting we will see how well you do with us, you will lose your virginity today"

Now that is what I am talking about, now back too biz. At that Indio speaks next

"We will be dealing drugs, guns, auto-theft and robbery and burglary only and each job must bring in over $3,000.00 or better we will not do nickel and dime crimes to get a bunch of time. They agree they will only do this when school is out during weekend, holidays and summer vacation, as they both explained, the women agreed that it was a master plan.

"But how will you deal with wars that are common among these crews in the hood and not have anyone identify we are the ones that have wreaked havoc on them or others"

Indio says "this will be the job of the assassins and not the crew when we get full security staff the assassins be called to assist if needed other than that they will be free to roam and keep eye on the crew" Their job as they were told would be just to ensure no harm came to the crew.

Chapter Seven:
The Virgin Killers

The meeting went well and so did the sex and the four of them were surprised that this young killer could handle himself in the bedroom and while they had to show him how to eat pussy it was no time before he was doing it like a pro. It did not hurt that he had to practice on four females who thrive off this and the dream of his life that will be a notch in his belt.

Pryce had them take him to his job in Park Slope; they were all shocked to find that he was actually working on a real job. However, he was not worried about what they think because he had to face his boss with a swollen eye, and the ride not only allowed more sex in the back seat but it also left him drained and ready to avoid work but Mr. Kim would only come to the house and get him.

As he, pulls up to the store, Mr. Kim and other storeowners are outside talking and as usual, Pryce is on time. Nevertheless, before he gets out the car he tells them to pick him up

"Yo pick me up at 7pm that is when the store closes" Pryce says as he staggers out the car and Mr. Kim sees him as he does so Marisol grabs him and gives him a long passionate kiss that has everyone on the street looking and one person walking by says "hey Let him breathe"

Pryce walks past Mr. Kim

"Hey Charles"

Pryce is the only one that calls him by his first name even the store owners do not call his first name, as he enters the store his son August comes running out the back with his toys, "Darrell Darrell time to play" "No my little friend I must first do some work then we can play, Pryce says. However, Daniel is not having any of it, Mommy Daddy tell Pryce to play with me. However, his father agrees with Pryce that he must work first then he can play with him. Mr. Kim still has not noticed that Pryce eye is swollen, but his wife does and asks him what happen to him as Pryce explains about the fight. As he continues to stock the shelves and put fresh fruit and vegetables on the stand in front of the store, delivery trucks pull up in front of the store and Pryce has to unload more sodas and food items. However, just as always Pryce works alone and he is quick with unloading the food and other items from the trucks, which is why Mr. Kim likes him so much because Pryce works hard and dedicated student of the arts as taught by him. Even though Mr. Kim does not recognize it, Pryce is working harder because his mind is on his next day of school.

However, unfortunately, Mr. Kim who asks him what happen to his face interrupts this thought

"I had a fight, but I was not the aggressor only on defense"

'So how did it start," Mr. Kim says like a father scolding his son

"I and a guy in my class had words and even though I thought nothing more of it, he had other ideas once we got to the lunch period"

"So he was upset by what you did or said"

"Yes I told him that he was lucky that most that stand in my way do not live to tell about it, and he took offense to it"

"So if your face looks like that how does he look?"

"Well let's just say that he is a sore loser, and this is not going to be over and that tomorrow we will be fighting again."

"So tell me about the boy and the fight you have gotten into"

"Well the second in command for the hardy boys is one of the biggest in my area and most powerful, but his lost places his rank in jeopardy since I am the thorn in his side the only way to get rid of it is he must get rid of me or win our next fight".

"So are you willing to let him win the next fight," Mr. Kim asks but he knows that his student would not let him or anyone else win just to satisfy them.

"No it will only give him and his friends' power they do not deserve"

"I see, so you must never be the aggressor, but always ready to defend when they are not, now get back to work"

"My work is finished; all I have to do is sweep

"So you do not consider babysitting my son a job"

"No, to parents its work but to people like not bound by all the parent rules. So your adopted son is going to spoil your biological son like grandparents do."
"I see and you think I should pay you for that"

"Why not you do it anyway," walks off towards August who is coming out the back with his mother.

Hey my little friend ready to go out back and play, as soon as August heard this he runs towards the back of the store and Pryce runs behind him and all his mother and father do is smile at how happy their son is. His wife knows that her husband and Pryce have a secret bond that involves the other side of his business. This also has to do with Mr. Kim teaching Pryce the arts that has lasted for the past three years and continues as each weekend he trains his student for three or four hours. She has no idea how her husband thinks she knows, but one thing for sure the family is pleased with the young black kid from the projects.

She remembers the first day they came across Pryce while he was still living in Red Hook projects, him and his friend were looking for a job and while they did not hire his friend Mr. Mrs. Kim took an instant liking too Pryce and how he worked.

From day one, they had a loyal employee, during the summer either Pryce would be waiting on them or during the winter, he would come straight from school.

While this is what Mrs. Kim sees, her husband sees that he has trained a killer in the most rigorous way using all types of techniques of torture that were passed off as sparing injuries. This strengthened his resistance to police torture tactics, and anyone else that sought to pry a statement from him. However, with this came firing guns grenades and other artillery that he will someday use in battles that have meaning not just for fun, no one knows the arsenal that he has buried within the floor of his bedroom. But these are his tools of the trade, his wife has no idea that Pryce has killed over 40 people and has over $150,000.00 in an account set up by Mr. Kim for college if he ever lives to go was Pryce words. However, Mr. Kim made him realize that, as long as his identity is in darkness he would survive when most hit man did not. Besides as Mr. Kim put it to him, who would think a kid was a hit man for the Korean mafia and as time went on the more Pryce realized that his boss was correct.

It was a typical workday for Pryce outside of the traffic at the last minute to but fresh vegetable and fruit before the store closed, it was a good day as always when he got the chance to play with Mr. Kim son who loved him as if he was his brother. However, while he was cleaning up his bodyguards came into the store, and it made his boss nervous but Pryce quickly explained that these were his friends.

All could see set him at ease, what he did not realize was Charles was examining the strangers, despite Pryce insistence they were friends. One of them made Ms. Kim nervous and she had to tell Pryce about it first chance.

She was talking about Mario and the older person that came with him, as she whispers to her husband and tells him what she feels about them. Charles trust his wife of twenty years, she has always been their when he least expected her to be and always had clear insight into matters that somehow slipped past him. He calls Pryce into the back office; the look on Pryce face reveals this is not good. When Mr. Kim calls him into the office it is always about work. As he heads to the office, Pryce looks at Mrs. Kim; her attention is on someone, just not Marisol. He enters and closes the door, the office for a fruit and vegetable stand is a little to extravagant for Pryce especially a fruit and vegetable stand.

"Ok what is going on, who I gotta kill?"

'Nobody yet but tell me about the two men that came into my store?"

'Well as you know I just moved into the neighborhood, and really cannot tell you anything about them why what is wrong?"

"One or both are informants and you need to be real careful with what you say around them, alright are you listening to me?

"Do I not always when it comes to this, thank you it will be a long quiet ride home?"

As he closes the door after exiting, he leans back on the door to reflect on what Mr. Kim just told him and Ms. Kim sees the exasperated look he has.

She could not help but wonder if the events of today are taking their toll, at such a young age he has to deal with so much when most kids are partying and enjoying life he is a contract killer and nobody knows it Pryce had to find out the truth one way or another.

On the ride home Pryce is quiet while Mario and Sylvester DiAntonio, a medium build Italian age 25 a lot older than those in the car even Pryce, was a friend of Mario but as his uncle told him birds of a feather flock together or like him and Indio say Evil minds think alike.

These two are dangerous and Pryce has to wait until they are gone before he asks questions about them, but in his mind, there is not time like the present. So as they come across Eastern Parkway they pass the big library that is illuminating the night skies, with the bright lights out front and the drive is relatively easy going as those that are on the road are either going home or to work the city never sleeps well with what he just heard neither will he.

"Hey Mario how you two meet up with each other"

"Why you need to know that?"

"Marisol pulls the car over" as she does, Pryce turns around in the front seat.

"Look when you in the car with me and I have no idea who you are or what your about then yes I need to know this and never as long as you live ask me a question with a question"

"Who the fuck you talking too like that" with that Pryce reaches in his bag and pulls out his 44 automag and points it at Mario

"Now who the fuck you talking too, ok look strip"

"What!" Both exclaim at the words but Marisol intervenes

"You heard him strip or I'll kill you in the car" they begin striping when she pulls out her 45 automatic from under the seat of the driver's side. Once they begin stripping, in the crowded car, Pryce tells her to turn around and head to Prospect Park. She makes the turn and as they head to the park, they drive through the park and once in a secluded area, he orders her to stop.

"Now get out, see you back in the hood"

For New York the September night is cool and has a slight frost in the air, that is the least of their worries two white looking people walking around naked in an all black neighborhood is not good for their careers. When they pull off, Pryce ask them Marisol and them to give him the 411 on them.

"Everyone expects that Mario is working for Five-O, but the other was just released after being caught with 5kilos of heroine"

"So basically they cannot be trusted, we need to keep Mario close to us in order for us to find out for sure if he is working or has been turned by the police."

"How do you intend on doing that when you just made the man walk naked into the streets and he look white"

This does not bother Pryce in the least; he has just too much going on in his head to worry about how some snitch is going to like what he just did to him. However, because Mario blew what he asked them out of proportion and he refused to allow anyone to speak to him in the manner he did without repercussions. The rest of the ride home was quiet and sex free, which would not be a bad idea but only Pryce just did not have the strength to do anything.

Chapter Eight:

"The Hood Made Me the Streets Approved Me"

The year is 1980, scarecrow has been out of the projects for three years now, and his new neighborhood is full of Italians, Sicilians, Puerto Rican, and four black families his makes five.

On the other side of the city, is where he once lived and now his childhood friends are coming to pay a visit. The Red Hook projects was scarecrows home and the adjustments he has had to make in this neighborhood, is a lifetime experience for him and while his other siblings have adjusted. Scarecrows adjustment is something his friends or family would never imagine, that this young skinny kid weighing 50 pounds soak and wet was really a hired gun for the Korean mob. As Scarecrow waits on his friends to arrive he is thinking if he should tell his friends what he is doing, but in his mind knows family and friends would never believe it.

Saturday morning and unlike the area, where scarecrow now lives the projects are just coming to life, with the partygoers just rising and the shoppers already moving. Fort Hamilton Parkway traffic is light for now, as Jeffrey and Gumby wait for chance to cross, the traffic light turns red and gives them a chance to move to the other side. Gumby muses to himself, that in life we move from one side of the street to the next and in life we move from one event to the next sometimes we wait for the light and at times, we do not. They move to the other side of the street as the light has held traffic, but in Gumby mind, this light cannot hold life at a standstill. As they move with the other pedestrians, under the by-pass where he can hear the vehicles above moving faster than he ran across the street.

The underpass is made of old brick and even the streets are showing its hidden treasures of the past, the trolley car tracks were only buried in the asphalt and now over the years the constant traffic and weather conditions have allowed the treasures of the old city life to show its face in the ground. Even the steel Pillars that are holding up bypass leading to the Brooklyn Battery Tunnel are showing signs of times gone by and need for upgrade as rust settles in.

As they approach the train station, they stop to buy two sodas from candy store. The train is adjacent to the diner, which is next to the candy store. This restaurant has seen more fires than matches in a matchbook, and just like the gas station across the street has seen as many owners as it went from Mobile, Shell, and now Texaco.

Inside train station, the lighting is dim and place smells of mold and piss, with token booth on the left and the turnstiles and exit gates on the right. They jump the turnstile and the token Booth clerk yells

"Pay your fare"

However, they both say

"Hell no"

It takes two escalators to reach the train platform, and the only light in this area, is the sunlight and if not for that. Then the area would be in total darkness, and despite the age of the windows and the dirt that has been present from for well over 50 years Gumby thinks to himself "maybe one day they will clean them" just not today. They have stopped in this area and Gumby is looking at the waterway that is under the train station, and he sees a tugboat moving on the other side of the waterway heading this way and knows that eventually the traffic will come to a halt, as the boat will pass under the train station and bridge opens up. His thoughts, are interrupted by Jeffrey who pulled out a bag of weed and begins rolling it up, and after lighting it he offers it to Gumby

"No thanks Jeff too early for me"

"No prob Gumby more for me"

"You were hoping I'd say no just greed Jeff"

Jeffrey is Gumby and scarecrow best friend, but out of the three of them Jeff is the only light-skinned person who is still friends with them others have but either they were too bossy or had other motive. However, who would ever think, that the motives of the old friends they have parted ways with, would now be there motives.

As the F-train pulls into the station, it comes to a stop and as the passengers exit Jeffrey pick pockets one of them as he exits the train. Smith&9th street is one of the oldest train stations in the city built before Gumby, Scarecrow or Jeff was born, and doing something the three of them will eventually do and that is show signs of aging but as for now, the youthful appearance is still fresh on them.

Once on the train one woman grabs her son very tight and Jeffrey responds after he sees her do that

"Bitch nobody wants your baby you think I am a pervert dam lady I'm only 14"

Gumby looks to see what has his friend all riled up, and sees that the woman has a death grip on her child that even the expression on the Childs face says he wish his mother would let go because he is hurting from her squeeze. However, apparently, Gumby is not the only one who sees this, and the other woman on the trains speaks up

"Look let the child go your hurting him, and besides those boys are just babies."

As the ride on the train continues Gumby goes back to his daydreaming, and now its Jeffrey turn to think of the time that has gone by since he has last saw his friend scarecrow. That one joint is the only thing that relaxes Jeffrey, strange that at his age he is now getting high to escape the nightmare of his friend molested by a boy twice his age in the neighborhood. While he stood and watched, the guilt comes not from him not helping but the fact that he was the one who allowed this to happen when he took scarecrow into this man home knowing what the man was going to do. That is only part of the story, nobody knows that for the past six, or more years this man has been molesting Jeffrey the only one that he has not lured into the house was Gumby.

Jeffrey is the only one who knows what happened to scarecrow and he remembers his vow that when he gets older that he would kill that man for taking away his youthful innocence with the rape. No none in the neighborhood knows, why Anthony was murdered. His body found yesterday after missing for four days, in the stadium bleachers with a dildo in his mouth, his penis cut off in his hands, and the words wrote in his blood "You will hurt no more children"

Therefore, when he found out he was dead he knew the only person that would have done this was, his friend scarecrow and now he will see the killer of his nightmare face to face, the only person who shares his pain. What he does not know is how this will change what he has done and really want to tell scarecrow, and today he promised that he would tell scarecrow today what he did and to thank him for doing something he was too much of a coward to do.

The quite time alone on the train, allowed the ride to go by quickly and as the train pulls into Jay Street Borough Hall, which is downtown Brooklyn and famous for Junior's restaurant and their Cheesecake and shopping. The other train they need is on the other side waiting for them, so they make a dash for the steps to reach train before its doors close. Signs of true New Yorkers, which know the trains well enough that they realize the trains only wait no more than five or ten minutes once, they enter station. Apparently, this train is on time and has a few minutes to wait, but as they board the train, Jeffrey steps in between the cars, removes the money from the wallet, and throws it on tracks. He gives Gumby$150 and he keeps $200 for himself.

Once they enter train, it appears as if the train was waiting on them because the doors close once they enter. Jeffrey sees a woman trying to catch the train so he holds the doors like most New Yorkers do and allows her to get on. At the other end of the car are two Guardian Angels, who now are the self-proclaimed police force for the city. The train car is full of shoppers and others going to work. A bum is sitting across from Gumby and Jeffrey, with four bags containing his whole life, looks at Jeffrey, and says.

"You wrong for what you did to that boy, and he was your friend some friends you are you need to tell him or you scared he will kill you like he did him, dirty niggas"

The entire train is laughing but Jeff is not, because what he said has a lot of truth to it and the only thing is that only three people in the world knew what happened and one of them is dead.

Even Gumby is clueless as to how deep those words have penetrated his friend; on top of that, this bum just blew his high with a few little words. All Jeff could do as a comeback

"Is that why you living in the streets"

In addition, the bum repeats the words again

"You wrong for what you did to your friend taking him in that house"

Which enraged him even more?

" look shut your mouth before I kill you"

With that, the bum and all the other passengers became deafly quiet. To the point all you could hear, is the train rolling on its tracks and sound vibrating on the walls. Even Gumby notices the tone in his friend's voice and has a bewildered look on his face. The bum continues with his antagonistic views

"Hell you don't have the balls to kill me or the man that hurt you, so stop faking"

When Jeff pulls out the gun, even Gumby is shocked, and one of the passengers who he will come to meet is at his side trying to help Gumby calm Jeff down.

As train pulls into the station and stops, his friend has gone into such a tirade with the bum that Gumby and another young Hispanic male had to pull him off the train. To Gumby this was déjà vu all over again, the last time he saw his friend lose his temper he destroyed an entire gas station by killing the owner and those who were getting gas, in a big orange ball of fire. That left bodies unidentifiable, so when he sees Jeff with a gun in his hand, going towards a man who ended his life years ago, he knows now is not the time or the place to add to his body count, Gumby is still trying to calm Jeff down, and the other teenager offers to help.

As the train pulls into the station, Gumby notices that it is their stop; he grabs Jeff by the arm and says

"Yo it our stop put the gun away"

In addition, the Hispanic person adds to it

"Yeah b too many eyes take a chill pill"

The voices brought him back to reality, but he has the look of a man who just came back from a psychotic episode. As he sticks the gun back under his shirt, the train comes to a stop and they exit, he looks back at the bum who is not looking at him. When he looks at the woman in front of the bum he notices urine on the floor, and it did not come from the bum but the woman sitting in the chair, in Jeff mind he says

"Dam she was so scared that she pissed on herself"

The train stops and they get off, and just as quickly as they do, it seems as if the passengers closed the doors because of how quickly they closed. As the train begins, moving Jeff is looking at the faces on the train car as it speeds away. It appears odd a person would go into such a tirade about what a man, who has no home or life, could have possibly struck a nerve that bad the boy was willing to kill for those words, but as with all things, Jeff knows that a hit dog will holler.

They walk upstairs and bid farewell to their new friend whose name, no one got but the air, who ask Gumby

"Yo B you need my help or got this?"

Gumby tells him in exhausted tone

"No, got this my partner will be here shortly"

He walks off and goes through the gate, Jeffrey goes to the bathroom, and Gumby is on the other side of the gate and goes to the phone to call scarecrow that is outside talking to Frankie

"Yo what's up Pryce, what's going on b?"

"Indio wat chu' doin trying to hit a lick"

Frankie "aka" Indio is 15 years old, 5'10", slim build and Puerto Rican, but looks Indian, another sure sign that the native Indians traveled the land of this nation long before the English settlers came to this country, and because of his Indian look, they call him Indio.

"No dats not my style you no dat Pryce, just trying to keep ol'boy from smokin a bum on da train"

"Word b who you talking bout"

"Dem two over dere "

He points in the direction of Gumby and Jeffrey

"Word those my boys from my old hood"

Scarecrow call out to them

"Yo Gumby, yo red WATS wit you two trying to smoke a bum on the train

As they explain to him what happened, Indio is still standing by listening to the conversation. When it was over scarecrow introduces them to Indio"aka" Frankie

"Yo Gumby, Red this my friend Frankie everyone calls him Indio"

Frankie looks at Jeffrey

"Yo everything kool now, dat bum had you heated no need to waste good bullets on a bum"

Jeffrey tell him

"No I'm good should not have let that bum get me heated like that"

They all exit the train station. In front of the station lies, a small newsstand that looks like if a strong wind came along it would blow away the entire stand, and behind that is a parking lot that is for those with cars who refuse to be burden with finding parking in the city while trying to be at work on time. As they turn to the right of the newsstand they pass another area of parking for the city workers, this lot is much bigger than the one behind the newsstand. New York City traffic, from Monday through Friday is chaotic and a true New Yorker who has a car would not dare not find parking in the city and fight the traffic if they intend on being to work on time. Today the cars that are in this lot are by those shopping in the area stores on city-line in Brooklyn. This block with old brownstone and aluminum sided homes, and fine trimmed hedges out front. Nevertheless, looking back behind them is another world that all but Frankie knows well too often of the red brick prison they call projects in New York City. What scarecrow or Indio does not notice is that Gumby and Jeff are glancing unnoticeably behind them at the projects behind them and wondering if they are perhaps going the wrong way.

At that instance, Jeff heart rate begins to beat faster, because in his mind he thinks scarecrow knows that he set him up and now will kill him as he killed Anthony. He begins thinking of ways to attack him when he approaches him, the pjs made them and now he will finally get to see if the streets will approve him for killing someone who had him sexually abused.

That is why the world that is behind them called the projects is still where he lives in his heart. Nevertheless, what his friends will soon figure out is that scarecrow is the most dangerous killer in this area fear by all who know him personally.

The projects may be behind him but everyday he wakes he sees them in front of him, and has many ties in those projects as if he lived in them just as long as he lived in Red Hook.

They say curiosity killed the cat, but curiosity sure could not kill these four. Each one notices the change in demeanor, clothing, and speech. Which is why, scarecrow has now just learned that the dirty ones are all over the city and even in his old hood. On the vest that Gumby and Jeff are wearing are the words Dirty Ones Brooklyn chapter F.T.W., those few letters could and are translated into so many different forms that only one has true meaning for scarecrow Fight to Win, all the others are just oppressed feeling of those who have no sense of direction.

On the corner down from the Grant Avenue train station, is a bodega [store] with Spanish music playing loudly, old men out front playing dominoes and women and children speaking a language Jeff or Gumby have not heard before. The only ones who seem to know what is going on is scarecrow and Indio. They see scarecrow speak to two people in the language they have never heard before, and they laugh at whatever scarecrow told them. Then come over to shake their hands, one ask who is so skinny he looks like the poster child for save the children and ask.

"Any man that will kill a bum over words is my friend all day every day and especially when they are friends of Pryce"

Both Gumby and Jeff are confused at the name they just called, they know they are friends of scarecrow they know not who this person Pryce is. Only Gumby was as he figured brave enough to ask

"yo scarecrow you friends with Pryce'

Indio and the others look at Pryce and Indio says aloud

"Scare crow" he might be a crow a real black crispy one at that but scare he is not" no your friend is Pryce.

Gumby and Jeff look at each other and recognize that the way it sounds as if their old friend is top dog in a hood where virtually no blacks exist, to them in their minds this is not possible especially for scarecrow. The one that to them is afraid of his own shadow is now top dog and the white folk love him, and the Germans. This is a title for the Spanish because those who do not speak Spanish say they are speaking German, on Rikers Island this is what they call Spanish people.

After Indio and the other boys leave, Gumby says

"Looks like we all got a lot of explaining to do"

After scarecrow sighs, he says

"You right so let's go to the house and we will talk"

As they continue walking Jeff, ask

Hey scarecrow is we going the right way, because all I see are a bunch of white people and they don't look friendly, the pjs back the other way and it's a long run to get help from our people"

At that scarecrow just laughs

"relax you two this my hood and these my peeps, you good as long as you remember the rules you steal from us loose a hand kill one of us lose your family"

At that, Gumby had to respond

"Look scarecrow so anytime we come in this neighborhood all we got to say we come to see scarecrow"

"No tell them you come to see Pryce, scarecrow do not exist anymore, that was the pjs this not the pjs the pjs on the other side as you see. Oh and tell no one in the pjs what you have seen or heard today, are we clear"

They look at him quizzically

"I said are we clear, the life you save will be your own"

They both respond, with a quiver in their voices

"Yeah sure old friend"

Now it was scarecrow turn

"What is the deal with those vests that you have on leave out no details,"

That one simple remark has them both confused, but Gumby is the only one who has confidence in his friend to know that whatever, it is scarecrow has assembled it will be in the best interest of those involved. He is only surprised to see that the people qualities that his friend had in the pjs is now on full display for the other side of the world to see. As Gumby muses to himself, it is one thing for just one ethnic group to like you and your qualities, but it quite something different when you have embraced all nationalities and merged them to follow you as scarecrow has done now. To Gumby nothing has changed, scarecrow was always the one to lead, he always had people that would advise him on matters and then he would decide on the best plan for everyone, and even if one disagreed, he would find a way to fit that idea into whatever it was he had planned.

They stop in front of a brownstone two-unit house, as he pulls out the key Gumby sees his childhood sweetheart come out of the house and knew from that point on they was in the right place, scarecrow, sister was 5'7" and looked to have gained five more pounds no more over the years. When they see each other all they could do was smile

"Well, well if isn't old Gumby and lil red robin, what brings you out the slums into the suburbs"

Gumby is still gawking at scarecrow sister

"Your brother brought us in to see him for the weekend, you going to be here all week with us"

"No got better things to do with my time than to hang around a bunch of thugs"

Gumby looks surprised she said that

"Why you call me a thug, I am not a thug"

As she walks over to him and sensually touches his vest

"So what is this, in the pjs this would be appropriate but in this area it is not and besides moms works for the NYPD and we know everything that you boys are doing or have done"

They all look bewildered at scarecrow sister comments about his mother working for five oh, is a slang term for the police. Scarecrow house is connected to other Brownstone homes and across the street is homes with aluminum siding, the person who developed this area created a blend of old and new homes with panoramic feel to it that while some may be afraid to admit, compliments the side of scarecrow never knew existed. At that scarecrow, ask his sister

“Hey where you going to grandma’s

“Yes will be back at 6 you gotta come get me!”

“Okay just call when you ready to go, you got the number to the block”

The phone on the corner of their hangout spot is for them to receive calls, and all those who answer it will always relay message. As she leaves Eddie is watching her leave, and Jeff tells him

“That is over with Gumby, no more childhood sweetheart”

They go inside, in Gumby mind she still wants him just as he wants her and when she turns around and blows a kiss at him he smiles and goes into the house.

Its 12noon, they decide to go to the ave and have pizza. The area consist of a 5&10, C-town supermarket, two jewelry stores, clothing stores, drug stores, foot doctor, old closed down movie theater, two pizza shops. The one they go to, is scarecrow and the rest favorite spot, because not only is the pizza good but the old man and scarecrow are good friends after stopping two people from robbing his store.

Now the ninety pound soak and wet kid from red hook projects has by other people account three bodies under his belt, but ask Indio and others they stop counting after the first four. Nevertheless, the most satisfying killing was the man who molested him and continued molesting his friend red robin ‘aka” Jeffrey. Which is why he does not understand why Jeff did not kill him, and what is even more confusing Anthony told him that he paid for others and me and when asked whom he paid, no answer was forth coming,. All he did say was that it was one of your friends, who you trusted most and with that, it is still hard for him to believe Gumby would do that to him and he would confront him today. Today is scarecrow judgment day, cleaning out the closet looking for peace in his life after the tragedy of molestation.

The shop is small, with a counter on the right for people to eat, on the left is Mr. John his friend preparing pizza dough, when he sees scarecrow and in broken English calls out to him

"Hey Pisano"

"Hey Mr. John, how are you today, can me and my friends get a pizza with extra cheese and sausage and large root beer to stay"

"Hey look crazy, why you know say the usual, you not eat here everyday"

Begins speaking in his native language and scarecrow peeps back behind him and walks back to him and whispers

"Oh wash your hands"

They laugh as Mr. John grabs him by the neck and then let him go after scarecrow; give him a hug as if they were father and son from another mother and brother.

Scarecrow finds a table in the corner and they sit down. While talking, some more kids come into store and go to video games on right from where they are sitting.

All the things Gumby could do is smoke not refer but cigarettes and scarecrow asks

"What else beside the vest do I need to know about?

Gumby and Jeff look at each other, and Jeff leans on the table with his elbows and in a soft commanding voice

"You first"

As scarecrow looks him directly in his eyes with the demeanor of one who is in charge

"Fair enough, what do you wanna know?"

Jeff says

"Well you can start by telling us why all of these people love you as if you were the king of Brooklyn"

"I am the most loyal person and assassin in area, and have the mob backing me put it like this they call I answer"

Jeff does not believe it as he looks at his friend and says

"Cut the bull shit you and I both know you would not hurt a fly, so what's the real deal"

"Really" scarecrow tells Jeff, "you know the old scarecrow not Pryce that is the big difference, and Indio, he my right hand man"

The tone made Jeff lean back and look at his friend in a completely different light, and it shocked him so much that he was at a loss for words that Gumby had to step in and get all the details of his childhood friend.

"What happen?" How why I mean so you're a hired gun for the Italian mob, so that old man must be your connec."

"No he's not, we became good friends when I killed two black dudes while they were trying to rob him and since then all the Italians in the area give me respect and the keys to the hood"

"so how does or where does the hired gun come into play, all I hear that you provide protection one time and they open and give you the keys, no way what is missing"

"you ,yeah I do not do work for them but others and that is what you don't know and will never know who, the respect and the keys come from the fact that just like we did not let people come in the hood robbing our people the same rule applies in this area, same strokes just different folks"

Gumby realizes from his friend tone that he truly is the boss, and see that same glare on his face when his friend has control over a situation, ands knows that one thing scarecrow does not like is for things not to be under control. Therefore, now it was scarecrow turn,

"Now what is going on with the vest?"

Gumby continues talking.

"Well first we are now part of the dirty ones they took over the old abandon dentist office, fixed that up and that is where they meet and party."

Scarecrow is amazed at the change Gumby has made, the friend he knew and loved was the one who betrayed him, and in scarecrow mind killing him would cause a war between him and the dirty ones. A war that no one needs at the moment but it is nonetheless very much necessary for vindication of the innocence that Gumby took from him. Scarecrow keeps the conversation going

"So how long and oh yeah two questions one how long you been down with them, two what was deal with the gas station and three the bum how did you let a bum get you that bent out of shape and what did he say"

Now Jeff has come back to life

"The gas station was just me losing my head, and we have been part of the Dirty Ones for three years, now the bum he kept telling me I was wrong for what I did and that I needed to tell my friend what I did"

This has scarecrow confused

"What did you do and who did you do it to?"

"I have no idea what he was talking about, thought he might know something about the gas station."

Gumby and scarecrow would be good poker players because Jeff could not read their faces that would have been an indication that not one of them believed his story, even scarecrow is having second thought that Gumby is the one who took his manhood and that it was Jeff Anthony was really talking about. Nevertheless, after Gumby smokes his cigarette, they leave, and as they get set to go outside a Chinese person, about 6'1" comes into the pizza shop and hands scarecrow an envelope and the only one who saw the transaction was Mr. John as always because if scarecrow were not in the shop the envelope would be given to him. Just as fast as it is to him he quickly gives it to Mr. John who places it in the rear pocket of his pants, and even while the whole shop is still oblivious as to what the skinny black kid and the Old Italian man have going on. The worker Joe is 6'1" 350lbs and scarecrow, help in the shop. The mob is paying Joe but what scarecrow is doing is out of love and respect for the old man and his hood. Something money cannot buy, and when he told the top mob bosses he met after this crime that this was his reason for doing so they quickly put all ill feelings for blacks aside and allowed him to move freely in their area.

As they exit, more teenagers are in front and Alphonso'aka'Bad Boy who is 15 years old 260lbs size 14 shoe at 6'2" pushed scarecrow in the back and falls into Gumby, he turns to face them and asks.

"Which one of you ducks as niggas pushed me?"

But Bad Boy thinking that his size over matched scarecrow killer mentality responded in a bold and brazen manner

"Me why you feeling Froggy duck ass nigga"

It takes scarecrow three seconds on how to figure out how to knock this goliath out, so when he draws back, he puts all his strength into his punch for a man weighing 100lbs and when he connects, he lands Bad Boy straight on his back.

Before Bad Boy gets up, Indio steps in between them and tells Bad Boy

"Yo chill B if you got beef with Negro you got beef with me ya heard"

But Bad Boy in his rage of a skinny niggas doing that to him, does not want to hear anything/

"Yo Indio you bugging B this duck ass niggas snuffed me and you telling me to let this slide?"

Indio gets in his face

"No you bugging all you need to do is play your position or me and you got beef so waz-up"

Bad Boy looks at scarecrow and Then Indio

"A'ight we gonna see each other again"

Scarecrow has wry smile on his face when he asks Indio

"One of your boys trying to get a rep"

Indio tells him

"Something likes that"

What scarecrow or anyone else notice was the mean grill Mario was giving scarecrow the entire time he was standing there, and Indio who did approached Mario after scarecrow and the crowd leaves

"Yo chec it Leave negro alone yo life yo familia depend on it ya heard no questions, no back talk telling you some good shit, keep him as a friend not enemy"

Indio walks off, which left an even more bitter taste in his mouth. The hate stems not from anything that scarecrow did to him, but it is the fact that scarecrow who just came to the hood is now well like and respected something he Mario have not been able to do since he lived in the hood especially with the Italians and then again nobody but Mario knows why.

Chapter Nine:

Get Me Out Of Here

Scarecrow is stirring in his sleep, after a long night with his old friends. The alcohol and the beer have brought the dreams he has tried to escape, but with his two childhood friends in the other room sleeping they do not know their friend is having nightmares and has had them every since he left the hood and the same words keep coming into his mind and dreams.

Knock, knock is anyone out there; I know someone is out there because I hear you. My how long did you think, it would be before I cried out hey! You act as if you are not paying me any attention ok! Ok! Listen to this "Get Me Out Of Here"

Call the judge, call the prosecutor and tell them this is not funny anymore "Get Me out Of Here" how long did you think you would keep me locked inside. What have I done to deserve this?

How long has it been, one hour, one day, one week, one month, well whose counting? A man in physical bondage counts days, weeks, and years. However, a man in mental bondage is oblivious to time and has no set release date.

Animals know that being stuck behind bars is not their original habitat. The food is foreign to them just as the imitation environment is, but at a glance, it is as if these animals have adapted. As man knows, prison is not his natural habitat and the foods have about just as much taste as a mud sandwich.

What kind of prison is this is it a physical prison where the body is confined but the mind is free. Look "Get Me out Of Here" There is no way a man mind is free but his body is not,

no such ideology in my world maybe it's difficult to understand, and maybe it's not hey "Get Me Out Of Here"

How can one be mentally free, when the very place that has him confined is censoring his speech? This what you call mental freedom, man has free will, and that free will allows man freedom of expression. Therefore, what are you waiting for "Get Me out Of Here?"

Wait, wait, maybe I should speak now or forever hold my peace. So I ask! Who is brave enough and patient enough to listen to all of my pain, yeah! Figured it out yet Know what your thinking is he free or not, can't get out and neither can you and truth be told don't want anyone in my world.

Prison is physical bondage, but nothing is worse than group of men who think they are mentally free. Nevertheless, have not figured out how to express thoughts to claim true mental freedom

Hold On, hold on, why are you walking away, hey stop "Get Me Out Of Here" because you're in bondage is this what you want for me "Get Me Out Of Here" today wait a minute I know what it is, the reason you don't hear me is my thoughts of speech are internalized and not external. Nevertheless, can you see the pain in my face?

Or are you truly mentally self-centered and mentally enslaved that all you see is your own sorrow, see it all over your face your saying the something as me "Get Me Out Of Here "So you can't free me when we both need help. So go on one day someone will "Get Me out Of Here" not you I guess.

As scarecrow rises from his bed drenched in sweat from the nightmare, he sits on the side of the bed with his head in his hands. His dreams and their meaning on hold as Indio and Angel walk into his room. The only difference between this dream and others is that Pryce has finally come to understand what the dreams mean and how to solve the problem that has a\haunted him for years. As always, Indio knows firsthand that scarecrow has dreams, but no idea what they are. As far as Indio knows, it is just from all the killing his friend has done over the years.

"More dreams Pryce, you need water or some more Jack Daniels, to get you going"

Scarecrow picks his head up

"No I'm good just getting my wits together, why are you two busters in my house so early"

Angel laughs at him

"What you think that since your friends from the other side of the city, gonna stop our routine now on your feet soldier we got people to see and places to go"

Pryce shakes his head

"You a crab angel, besides can't go got company and they are not going with us"

Indio tells him

"So leave them at the club and we can go on, the boys will take care of them"

The look on scarecrow faces, made Indio respond

"No we will leave that up to you, but if you will not we will do it for you. Besides, we talk to spanky he gave you the green light, not in the hood though and they must not find the body"

'All these rules on how I should kill, my enemy who will never mind, look tell them I make no promises"

Indio turns towards the door

"Look we will be at the club you got five minutes, or we will come and get you.

Angel jumps in

"Yeah it won't be pretty if we do'

They all smile as they head out the door. As they do, Gumby walks in

"Hey scarecrow kind of heard the conversation and need to know you talking about us.

The look on his friend face let him know that they were, and now Gumby heart is racing.

"Why did you call us out here to just kill us, what have we done to deserve death? You forget we were tighter than we were with our own brothers and sisters so why! WHY!"

Jeffrey walks in the room at that moment, and scarecrow grabs his 44magnum from under his comforter. It is 98 degrees outside and scarecrow has a down comforter on his bed when everyone else is using lighter sheets and blankets. When they see the gun, it changes everything about what was going on.

"Yo have a seat both of you, and keep your hands where I can see them please don't try me"

Jeff begins to reach

"Ok look"

Fires off one round that grazes him in the shoulder

"What the fuck is wrong with you Pryce, you crazy bastard"

"Told you not to move your hands and you did"

Gumby is shocked and quickly surrenders,

So you going to kill us in the crib, before you do tell us what we did"

"Not we Gumby you, you was my best friend and for. Well tell me this how much did it cost?"

"Cost what are you talking about?

Gonna play dumb, you got five seconds to tell me or they will find you in the Hudson River"

"I have no fucking idea what you're talking about scarecrow please tell me, PLEASE, PLEASE"

Ok since you wanna play dumb, Anthony how much was Anthony paying you and how much he gave you for me"

"You sick bastard, you think I would let that pervert touch my brother really scarecrow no you wrong, why you think that"

"When I killed Anthony he said my friend who was real close to me sold me out to him, so you was the only choice because nobody is closer to me than you"

"No sorry swear to god it was not me, but do know that red robin had been.

He stops mid sentence and looks at Jeff, and scarecrow notices the same expression and looks at him as well.

Gumby asks him

What is the deal Jeff, why did you do it? You tried to get me it did not work so you got scarecrow. "You sick bastard you betrayed us to a dam pervert. Oh my fucking god

Scarecrow notices the look on Gumby face as one of pure vengeance, like when he found out crazy Greg was beating him up and his friend came out of nowhere with a bat and began pounding Greg with the bat, and the only one who could stop him was scarecrow.

Before scarecrow could react, Gumby grabbed the gun from him and fired two shots into his chest. While they were not life, threatening he had to get Jeff out of the house before any one came home. Scarecrow tells him.

"You should have killed him; his life is not worth it"

"No he going to suffer more, and hell when the boys find out they are going to kill him"

, scarecrow tells him

"You missed most of the conversation; I have the green light to kill him and you"

Gumby facial expression changes

You still going to kill me

"No just him, forgive me I really thought it was you"

"How could you think I would do something like that, me of all people scarecrow?"

"Look when he told me that it was a close friend you are the only one who came to mind, listen we got to get him to a hospital"

They pick him up out the chair, and begin applying towels to the wounds to slow the bleeding down. Gumby goes in the kitchen, comes back with ice cubes, and wraps the ice cubes in the towel and scarecrow asks

"What is that for?

Gumby tells him

"To slow down the bleeding, now what are we going to do walk him to the hospital, in broad day light seriously"

"No, we going to call a cab, put him in the cab, drop him off a block away, and let him walk the rest of the way alone."

As he goes in the other room to call a cab, Gumby stays with Jeff and tears are in Jeff eyes

"Save the tears, you should have thought about that when you sold him out, my only question is why?

"Anthony told me if I didn't he would tell the hood what he was doing to me"

"So then your family would know about it"

The expression on Jeff face let Gumby know there was something more behind all this and he had to know

"What is going on, what else are you not telling me?

Jeff lets out a sigh, and as he does scarecrow walks in the room and listens at Jeff as he tells his story.

"My family knew, Anthony was my cousin"

Therefore, scarecrow asks him

"What do I have to do with that?

Jeff answers the question, which shocks them all

"I'm gay and he was going to tell everyone this, so I had to get one of you he wanted both of you and scarecrow was top of the list"

Therefore, I have to ask Gumby directs it to both of them

"When and how did all this happen?

"one day when scarecrow was selling fireworks, I told him Anthony wanted to buy some and took him to his house, when we got their he gave scarecrow a drink that made him dizzy, the same he gives to all his victims"

Now scarecrow is reliving the nightmare again, after hearing everything Jeff is talking about he remembers the day as it was yesterday. He recalls the drink but he also recalls Jeff leaving or as he begins to wonder now did he, he questions himself and since all parties were present he knew that he needed to get the answers while they are talking.

"so when you took me in the house you left after or before the drinks"

"No I stayed and watched the entire event, what nobody knows is that he kept pictures of all his victims, and they still exist. Antony made his money selling nude photos of kids he raped, and you were no different."

"In fact, Anthony was surprised those perverts fell in love with it, they were willing to pay big money just for one day with you."

Before he could respond, the cab blows his horn, to let them know the cab is waiting on them. All this day did was bring more questions than he had answers, for the trauma he endured over the years but if he was confused so was Gumby Not only was Gumby confused but heated over the news and he was not there to help him, but even more his friend did not tell him about what happened to him.

As they get in the cab, and Gumby slides in beside Jeff before the door closes Gumby asks him

"Why didn't you tell me, you didn't trust me?

Scarecrow just looks at him and gets in the cab and as it pulls off, he sees Indio and Angel coming up the block and scarecrow tells the cab to stop. When it does, he walks towards Indio and Angel and whispers to them what has just taken place. Nevertheless, to scarecrow surprise, Indio tells him something he should have known. That anytime anyone of them calls a cab it is for one of two reasons someone is either shot or they trying to get out of town, and since they knew Pryce was not trying to leave town they figured it had to be someone dead.

The cab stand is adjacent to their club they hang out in so when they call, immediately someone in the club is notified and someone is in the club 24 hours a day seven days a week they even have dispatchers on all shifts.

Therefore, to scarecrow it was no surprise, he also knew he was 20 minutes late and they were coming anyway. Just like Gumby was in his days, in red hook projects now, Indio was his most trusted and loyal friend just as Gumby was. To him this is all he will need to deal with the life he has chosen, and glad that it would take no convincing but only if his friend will not hold it against him for believing he was responsible for his rape.

As they ride across conduit Blvd going to Inter-boro hospital, they pass Burger King and a old gas station that looks as if it has seen better days, where all the paint is gone save for a few fragment that refuse to let go, just like the owner refuses to let go of his business he built with his hands. Just behind the old shop is a combination tennis court paddle and racquetball courts, belonging to the apartment complex with terraces called Linden Plaza.

These apartments have a mixture of welfare and working class families all paying different rent but receiving the same services such as 24-hour security. From Monday thru Friday, this stretch of highway and grassy knoll just to the left of the driver, is where those same people living in those apartments will cross this road to catch the train that will take them into the city for work, school or just for interviews, and scarecrow knows that his life is changing. All are amazed at how well he has adapted to his surroundings, with his reasoning, and partiality he takes no sides right or wrong, some call it a weakness, but to others that is death. Indio and others around him known that Pryce as they call him is one of the most youngest and dangerous killers of the hood, no one knows of the true side of this young killer but Indio who has seen him love and be loved by all, but with this comes hatred and jealousy which is beginning to stir.

As they make a right hand turn down a small patch of roadway, that leads them pass Linden Plaza which consist of five buildings three on one side two on the other. The two buildings are closer to them as they ride past them, the other three become hidden behind the two buildings as the cab comes to a stop and they let Jeff out they close the door and the cab pulls off. After making a U-turn, it quickly pulls off bringing the other buildings back into view, and Gumby breaks the silence

"hey brother why you didn't tell me, I would have been there for you have I not always been, if nothing I apologize for not being there with you when he came for you I should have went you forgive me"

As scarecrow turns and faces him

"It's not your fault, I should have told you and I also was wrong for believing you were responsible, you forgive me brother"

Gumby reaches out

"Dam right, the world is ours together let's get down to business"

The cab driver looks at him quickly

"Sounds to me Negro, we got help"

"You the driver what would you know?

The driver looks in the rearview mirror,

"Hey my name is Jerry glad to have you brother we heard a lot about you Gumby, just so you know I told him it was not you"

No one asked you, why did Indio send you anyway?

"I'm the best personal security you got; you just hate to admit it"

With that scarecrow quickly changes conversation, and as Jerry and Gumby talk scarecrow is deep in thought. Scarecrow knows Jeff will not live long, and wondered how long it would take.

None of this is important as the meeting that he is about to attend, one that will determine the existence of the E.N.Y. Dynasty and its credibility. No one knows that these young teenagers are preparing the path for the most clandestine gang ever seen.

Since Gumby wanted a bag of cess, Jerry takes us to Doscher& Pitkin Avenue as Jerry put it they have the best cess in the hood and the bags are fat. As we pull up to the shop which is a store front used by all drug dealers in New York as a legitimate business, we get out the car and go inside and the potato chip rack has four bags of chips on the rack, and only one soda in the cooler. The chips look as if they were here during the cave man times, the color on the bags are gone even the name of the chip company is faded. Scarecrow goes to the window, in Jamaican accent

"Yo Mon let I can I get a bag of dat cess Mon"

The person behind the Plexiglas sees scarecrow and responds to him.

"Daron a you dat Mon, cha when ya start smokin the ganja Mon"

"Nicademus bring ya bumba clod from behind the glass Mon, cha ya kno I smoke no ganja Mon this for my bredren right here so"

As nicademus come from behind the glass, he embraces scarecrow and Jerry, and after he introduces himself to nicademus, he has a grin on his face.

"Yo mon Daron told the dred all about you Mon, we finally get to see Gumby what they call him"

Before Gumby could respond scarecrow does.

"Do not answer that, the life you save could be your own"

"Yo mon tell us"

"They call him scarecrow"

Demus laughs, no one call him by his whole name unless you are the police or scarecrow, so everyone calls him Demus for short. What Gumby is trying to figure out in his mind is how this person fits into the whole scheme of things that scarecrow has going on, so far he sees that Jerry is his personal security and he knows the only ones that need personal security are those who have enemies larger than his bankroll. Gumby has his mind set, on finding out the extent of the operation that his friend has going on and a way for him to be right by his friend side for the entire time. Besides, in his mind he is the only one that will protect him as he has done from the pjs to now.

They are standing in front of the store, and across the street is a school and on the other side are more brownstone houses, only this time the architectural design is just one panoramic view of brownstones that blend perfectly with the school building that sits in front of them. Next to the store is a real candy store, which sometimes those in the hood get confused with the shop next to it as the weed shop. The more they talk the more Gumby is learning about what is going on with his friend, Gumby notices that scarecrow glances at him periodically and he senses scarecrow knows he is picking up on what they are talking about.

Gumby also knows that scarecrow is expecting a bunch of questions from him , but only the answers will not be coming from scarecrow but someone else that he is about to join on his security team.

From where they are at it is a straight shot to the cab stand and once they arrive, the welcoming committee is waiting for them and they go inside after speaking to a few of the girls out front.

"Hey Negro"

Marisol is 14 years old and Puerto Rican at 5'4" and has a crush on scarecrow, but only scarecrow does not like her he likes her girl friend. As young as she is, scarecrow finds it hard to believe that this young girl is already eating other females at a young age. Nevertheless, when he looks at Joan, the king of the dikes in the hood he understands, just as he understands that there is something more to Joan and Marisol just freaking on each other. He walks over to Marisol and Joan

"You really wanna do a three some with us"

At that Joan responds

"Why you scared, we might turn you out or have you on the walls like Spiderman?

"The only ones who will be climbing the walls are you two"

At that Marisol responds

"Our place at 7pm don't be late"

They walk off and scarecrow goes into the club and walks straight to the back.

The club is really a game room that has a pinball machine and six other arcade games that people are playing and three tables but two chairs for the tables, the counter is on the left next to the pinball machine and behind the counter is the cooler that has beer and soda. The office they are about to enter is straight ahead, and the bathroom is on the left of the office for all male and females. As they go in, there are no desk and only one table in the middle of the floor with seven people sitting around it, on the other side is a door where that leads Gumby could only imagine and about to find out. As scarecrow sits down, he calls Jerry

"Look take my friend to the crib and give him the 411 on what his job will be that's all he needs to know for now, Yo Gumby you good go with Jerry. Know you hungry see you in about an hour oh yeah arm him j"

Jerry heads for the door without even questioning or asking for approval, they already knew that only one of them would return to the projects and that this was supposed to be Jeff orders not Gumby. Jerry thought Jeff would be the one he was taking upstairs, not Gumby and he is glad that his thought was correct that it was not Gumby but Jeff. With the short time that he has had to talk to Gumby, he sees that Gumby is the one person outside of Indio that scarecrow trust with his life besides him. The only thing confusing to him and others is how Indio and Pryce became such good friends and where it all took place, because Pryce "aka" scarecrow has only been living in the hood for a year and a half the other was spent in Linden Plaza.

Everyone knows both go to school together, the bond that over the short time t has everyone confused and afraid, not of what they could do to each other but the damage they could do together. Everyone knows Indio reputation for a laid back quiet person, with a temper worse than the devil or god combined. In New York, if rush hour traffic has no compassion why should the streets. Nevertheless, Jerry knows Pryce and Indio redefined the rules of the game. What most calls weakness is the strong side of the neighborhoods two teenagers that someday the police and the world would know about and cringe? Word on the street is that these two are so bad not even the devil wants them, now his childhood friend has joined the ranks and what Jerry does not know is that Gumby is more dangerous than his friend.

At the emergency room At Interboro Hospital, the place is swarming with police from the 75th precinct one is outside the operating room waiting on the doctors to finish operating on Jeff. It is standard procedure that all gunshot wounds must be reported to the police, the only bad side for Jeff is that there was a drug war two minutes prior to him getting to the hospital. The Dirty Ones were in the fight and with that vest; Jeff was a prime suspect in the killing of six people and three children.

Under heavy sedation of anesthesia, Jeff mind is on why Gumby not scarecrow shot him but that is only one side of his conscious mind that tries to rationalize that what he did was not wrong. But with all conscious there are two sides and the side that finds fault with everyone except the person, the other side realizes that not only are Gumby and scarecrow good friends these two were basically born on the same day and in the same hospital. Only difference is that their mothers are not the same, in the pjs everyone says that this is why those two are so close because of the time and date of birth. Through it all, Jeff also understands that if he would have killed scarecrow Gumby was sure to kill him with no hesitation and the only reason why he hesitated on Gumby because of their close relationship and he would have same treatment, only afterwards he would have been dead not just injured.

Outside the doctor is talking to the Detective, who watches as they wheel Jeff pass him to a room for him to recover. The detective anticipates on talking too Jeff, but it might be too late for that to happen if the doctor diagnosis is correct the bullets that Jeff were shot with were laced with poison.

"Hey doc detective Samuels 75th precinct how is the Youngman?"

"Well if you have any intentions of talking to him that will not be possible"

"Why is that doc?

"The Youngman was shot with bullets that even if he lived the poison in his bloodstream would kill him slowly"

"I'm not following you doc"

"Look the bullets poisoned his blood stream and whoever did this knew that this would be a slow painful death, you see the bullets have been laced with a substance that will eat away his insides"

"Well do you know what it is, and can you give him something to reverse the effects"

"Yeah if he would have been shot and within five seconds brought to the hospital, and then we would have to be told what it was that was on the bullets and at this moment we do not have a clue"

"So when will you know?

"In about three days, and then it will be too late. The Youngman will not be able to hold his food he will be as they say [Loose in the caboose]"

"Thanks doc if you have anything else or find out anything else please call me"

After he hands the doctor his card, he walks out into the parking lot where his partner of seven years detective Frank Pasqual been on the force for 16 years and seven have been with Christopher Samuels. Detective Samuels unlike Detective Pasqual comes from a long line of family who have been police officers, in fact Samuels father is the Commanding officer for the 23rd precinct, uncle is the chief of the crime scene division, and brother is on the bomb squad. His grandfather shot in the line of duty, or so the story goes the truth is that he was when the dealer refused to pay for his protection. That sparked a citywide manhunt for the killer of the officer, some killers rather be carried by six than judged by twelve and Samuels grandfather killer was no different,

The only thing baffling Samuels now, is the only known survivor of the shooting just an hour ago is about to die from poisoning and this takes some real knowledge for a person to do this. Still more, no one knows what it is, and if that is the case, the next question will be who, and how did these people get their hands on this poison.

While scarecrow is in the next room, Gumby is amazed at all the weapons that Jerry showed him. In his mind, this is not what he expected his friend scarecrow to be into, to him scarecrow would be sitting in college or on his way to college to be a lawyer or corporate executive making millions of dollars. Times have changed and so has scarecrow or Pryce is the name they call him now, in the other room the future of the E.N.Y. Dynasty is being planned and alliance are being forged.

Joan leads the way with Indio, Pryce behind her wearing ski mask, from the look you would assume Indio, Pryce are Joan bodyguards and Moses bodyguards reach for their guns.

"Relax no need to get nervous they with me" the guards relax and move their hands off their guns.

The atmosphere of the meeting changed when the people with ski mask walked in. Moses and his boys had no idea who these masked men were; only problem was it was not all men but two men and 8 women and Joan did all the talking. Joan responds to the insults.

"Look respect us as we respect you"

Moses is 6'0" 20 years old and just finished doing 15 years in Clinton Correction Facility for murder, and the leader of the D.L. Boys one of the oldest gangs in the hood is quickly the first to speak out.

"No way are we going to join a bunch of dick sucking bitches surrounded by bitches wearing ski mask, to pay for protection from you"

Scarecrow laughs sinisterly at the words from Moses.

"Sorry that you feel that way, but apparently your people have not been keeping you informed of the changes that have taken place in your absence" Joan tells him

"Oh really what is that?"

He asks to none in particular, but scarecrow keeps staring at the two bodyguards behind Moses, and Joan leans over on the table with both eyes on Moses.

"Now what makes you think you're going to make it out of this room without falling in line?"

"What makes you think I will not?"

"You really are lost in the past, well welcome to the future"

At that instance, Indio shoots the two bodyguards and Moses has the look of one who knows that he is next.

"So you were saying, now you still wanna play hard to get"

"We could work this out, you know I been gone a long time and was not aware of the changes in the hood, what do you say ladies no hard feelings"

Joan is still leaning on the table

"The reputation you have makes we wonder if I really should let this go"

Joan knows Moses will not hesitate to kill her or her family, and for this reason the idea of letting him go never crossed her mind, Indio glances at his friend to determine if quite possibly his friend is considering this request by Moses.

With no signs of wavering, Indio adds another body to his kills and as he wipes his hands

"Yo Pryce your turn to clean up"

"No that's why we got them, gestures towards the door"

Hell you said you work for sanitation, well time to work"

"Only problem is I never said what area supervisors do not clean up when they have people to do so.

He calls for Angel, as he comes in the door all he could do is shake his head

'I love you two dearly, but for once try not to make such a mess have better things to do"

Indio asks quickly

"What may I ask is that?"

"I do have a love life"

"Ah angel, the hand don't count as a love life"

"Well when it comes from your sister it does"

With that, they all laugh as Indio and scarecrow walk out the room, no one in the room knew what happened because, the music was loud, and the gun had a silencer on it to muffle the sounds. The only thing that would let everyone know what happened is the blood on Indio and scarecrow shirts, and before they got out the door, Marisol stopped him.

"You two amateurs, real killers don't make a mess. Strip"

They look at her,

"You real freaky can't wait huh" scarecrow says

Scarecrow begins to unbutton his pants, and Marisol is shocked.

"Hey what the fuck are you doing?"

"You said strip," scarecrow says in an excited voice

"I meant the shirts, hope you this way later if not they can be ripped off you"

"Not into the S&M, but sounds real freaky to me little fore play NICE REAL NICE"

After they get the shirts off, they walk out the door as Marisol grabs a plastic bag from behind the counter and put the shirts in side. So now, Indio and Scarecrow walk down the street showing off the youthful physique to the girls on the corner, one of the girls make a comment in Spanish that translated into English means they stuck up bastards. To this scarecrows stops, and approaches the girl.

"Ma why you tripping on me like that, if you wanna get with me all you got to do is say the word"

With that, the girl sucks her teeth and rolls her eyes, as she looks him up and down checking him out close up.

"I don't wanna get with you"

As scarecrow leans over so she could smell his Egyptian musk oil, as he whispers so softly to her, he sees her breast moving up and down, as her breath gets harder and harder. The smell of his Egyptian musk oil and his closeness, made her pretend as if protesting she puts her hands flat on his chest, then with her well manicured fingernail outlines the contours of his chest with her finger and then Dolly takes a real deep breath and breathes out where Pryce could feel her breath on his chest.

"Yes you do just playing hard to get, like a challenge we need no introductions we know each other already, yo spread the word ma I'm your guy now ya heard"

He gently caresses her chin with his finger, as he moves in to kiss her gently on the lips.

"Ok, so where you going now that it"

"No," scarecrow says ever so softly. As Dolly girlfriends stand around gawking at the new kid on the block is just as sweet as he is deadly, all the girls were trying to be the first he chooses to be his girl, and he chose Dolly. They knew this gave them status in the hood as long as they were with Dolly. The girls knew that these two did not have a crew yet, but the word was they were in the process of eliminating all those who tried to form alliances with Hardy Boys. Some even said they were really trying to take over, not just the crew territory but the mob as well.

When scarecrow grabs her by the hand, and she follows they follow behind her. Her friends could see that her walk has changed; she is really strutting up the street holding on to his arm with style letting all see she was Pryce woman. As they reach the pizza shop, scarecrow and Indio eat, other girls are out in front of the pizza shop and when they see her, they turn towards her and him. As they approach the boys standing around dap Indio and scarecrow up, and the other girls hug and kiss them on the cheek and he turns to Dolly

"Going inside to get something to eat you hungry ma?

"Yeah," she says in a sweet sensual voice. At that scarecrow, turn to Mr. John who is at the window aye Mr. John give her something to eat and put it on my tab, and let me get the usual"

In broken English Mr. John, tell him

If you do like last time I cut your tongue out

'as long as you do not hit me with those bear claws, you pull out a knife any day on me"

This was a joke to some but scarecrow saw Mr. John slap a man with his hand and break his jaw, these hands look like he could play catcher for the New York Yankees without a catcher's mitt. Scarecrow goes inside the shop and head straight to the back office, those inside were shocked to see these two walk in and go straight to the back with no shirts on. Inside the office Ricky, was a known street hustler who made a dollar selling hot items and one of the things he usually sold was memorabilia of the New York Yankees, Ricky and scarecrow were true Yankee fans and scarecrow brought two Yankee shirts, and put one on as Indio looks at him scarecrow turns

"What!"

"So you didn't get me a shirt," Indio asks scarecrow

"Trying to buy pussy you don't have one" scarecrow smiles

"So who you gonna fuck first Marisol or Dolly" Indio asks

"Both" and scarecrow takes a seat. So let's get down to business, as they sit down Ricky sits to the left of scarecrow as they sit around a small circular table and Indio on his left. Ricky stands about 5'8" and the same physique as scarecrow slim at the waist and face with blond hair, and chain-smokes Marlboro cigarettes like he on death row.

"Okay how do we get inside the Jewelry Store? Scarecrow asks.

"Not to worry I have the entire blueprint for the store"

When Ricky spoke, his voice gave Indio the impression he was skeptical about doing this job just because of who was protecting store.

"What you have second thoughts about doing this job Rick?

"No not really",

Ricky was stuttering real bad and the bad part is the only time he did this was when he was nervous or scared, and his stuttering even made scarecrow lean over and put his hand on his shoulder.

"Look Ricky we been planning this job for a year and a half, no time to get cold feet now you hear me"

"No! However, it is just that, these people will not let it go they will hunt us down until they find out who did this and then kill all of us."

"How are they going to find out?" scarecrow asks

"Well you know people talk, and you know one thing leads to another" Ricky with a quiver in his voice

"Listen nobody knows about this but the three of us, so either you going to tell or one of us. So what do you know that you're not telling us?"

"L--o--o--k," the stuttering is getting real noticeable

"calm down Ricky, your among friends now listen to me real closely tonight we are going to complete this job and when it's over we all will be able to relax and enjoy the rewards"

He pats him on the shoulder, Ricky takes a deep breath, and when he breathes out.

"Pryce this is big time, nobody who has any sense would think of doing this, are you hearing me we are crazy"

"Well you said nobody with any sense; we three have no sense that is why we are doing this job. Besides who would think three 15 year olds would do something of this nature"

"Guess you right, man this shit crazy let's get these bastards"

"Now you talking, we will see you at 11 pm in front of this store, got it," scarecrow tells him

"Oh one thing Pryce, don't be late" the stuttering is gone but Indio is Leary about him and stares at him quizzically.

"Are you kidding me I am never late"

The look on Indio and Ricky face would let all know that being late to do a lick is scarecrow MO, to the point Ricky one time thought he got cold feet and just never showed up. One job he was already waiting on them, would be fine if it was just that one time but out the twenty odd licks they did, he was either late or already waiting on them. As they are about to exit, Mr. John comes into the back,

"Hey let me talk to you Pryce," Mr. John tells him and when Indio and Ricky stop, he tells them

" I want to speak to him alone"

Therefore, that queue they both leave them alone and the door closes behind them

"Hey have a seat and drink with me, they don't know you drink only I do"

Truth he was the only one that knew he got drunk, scarecrow would not drink with no one else but Mr. John, and this time would be no different. Each time he would drink, or want to drink is when he knew scarecrow was going to do something. However, on this night, the conversation was not the usual it was more serious than all the others were. What Mr. John knows nobody else should know?

"Look we good friends, and no want to any ding happen to yuze.'

The broken English was understandable but where this is going was not clear. This made scarecrow put down the drink and lean towards John.

"Stop pussy footing around and tell me what is going on you have always been straight with me so let's not change that"

John lets out a deep sigh" The Genovese know about the jewelry store, so the word is if you do it they will kill you and your family and anyone involved will die as well."

" tell Mr. Genovese you delivered the message, but also tell him that if he goes anywhere near my family the N.Y.P.D., F.B.I. organized crime task force will be shutting him and his entire operation down"

"So you are going to still do it? Even after what I told you"

"Yeah, threats only make me more brazen, now had he not did that then quite possible I would have changed my mind, but hell no" scarecrow speaks with indignation in his voice, about the threats he was just given and as he is talking two men walk into the office. Both no doubt to scarecrow are from the Genovese family, and came to deliver a message to him. One of them approach him,

"Hi my name is Vincent, and this my partner Salvatore we come to talk to you"

"No my friend John already gave me your message, got business to take care of but you can deliver this message to your people. Tell them this, if any one of you grease balls go near my family the entire NYPD, and the FBI organized crime task force will shut you down and I will come behind them and finish off what is left.

They look at him as if quite possibly he thinks this is a game, in all the years as mob henchmen nobody has ever sent threats to the family especially not a nigger. This really pissed them off and they did not hesitate to let him know it.

"Look you ungrateful nigger, when the Genovese crime talks you listen understood"

"No! You fucking grease ball and second get your paws off me or you will have cement shoes, now true the Genovese crime family is notorious but listen sometimes the ones you think care really do not now this the question who has more to lose me or the Genovese crime family?" Fuck with my family and every mob boss will be in jail before sundown,

With that, scarecrow and Indio walk straight out the pizza shop, after picking up their food and pass two other henchmen from the Genovese family waiting at cars outside. Salvatore is still shocked that this nigger was so disrespectful, but to him either he is bold or the jewelry store heist is a smoke a screen. All the tales about scarecrow/Pryce is his loyalty, to him and Bobby who is outside waiting this is not something he expects from Pryce who they have dealt with in the past. On other occasions once they told Pryce the family owned the business or had under its wing he backed off, despite their insistence to the others orders are orders and they had to come talk to him and the conversation has Vinnie upset because he still thinks he will rob one of the family stores.

Salvatore thinks to himself, only if he could talk to Pryce to find out for sure and go back to the family and assure them all is well but now he must wait until it happens. He knows this is not good for his ulcers, or high blood pressure, but it is his job and his life "Dam Dam" he says in his mind thinking about Pryce until Vinnie interrupts his thoughts.

"Still think the nigger is not serious"

"Yeah you have never dealt with him only me Bobby, and John has until you have. You will always have a negative vibe about him, trust me it is not the family and I will put my life on it. At that Mr. John agrees with him,

"Yes I will put my life on it in fact",

He says in his broken English accent, come this way. He leads them to the phone and picks it up, and Vinnie asks
"what you doing?"

"Calling tom," Tom Was a captain in the Genovese crime family and high ranked, him and John were close friends and while Tom knew nothing about Pryce, one thing he did was listen to John who was about to put his life on the fact that Pryce was not going to steal from them.

"Hello! Tom this John, yes listen Vinnie and Sal are with me now all me and Sal ask is that you leave the nigro alone he is not going to steal from the family me and Sal put our lives on it"

Not only did those words stun Vinnie but, Tom was speechless for five minutes before he responded to what John had just told, and Vinnie was just as shocked and began wondering who was this nigger that his friends were so reluctant to believe was about to steal from them. To Vinnie, niggers were not to be trusted and this one was no different, he just could not see any good in this nigger and despite what they say, he is determined to kill this nigger first chance.

Scarecrow is talking to Bobby, who before he left called him over. As they talk, the conversation gave Bobby the clear indication, it was not the family, but something more that prompted Bobby to ask

Look no B/S you always been straight with me" Bobby ask and scarecrow has a sly grin on his face which made Bobby grin as well and he knew the truth was coming just not all the details that most would give.

"Are you going to steal form the family?" the grin on Bobby face is gone as it is from Pryce face. Instead of answering the question, Pryce answers the question with a question.

"Do you trust me?" Bobby does not hesitate to respond

Dam right"

"Well then why would you ask me a question like that?" with that they shake and he walks off. Never let you down Bob not about to now do it now, scarecrow tells him as he walks off, the other person who is like Lou Ferrigno and the poster child for Body building magazine, Chris Santucci is quick on his feet and ranked number 3 in nation in martial arts. Even though he does not know Pryce personally, and just meeting him now allows him to believe that loyalty is important to him. Now he understands why Bobby speaks so highly of him, this black kid weighing no more than 80lbs soak and wet with two bricks in his back pocket, exhibits the loyalty the mob expects from its own people and here it is this kid is showing loyalty.

On the corner of Sheridan Avenue, sits a gray and burgundy Lincoln continental belonging to his boss Mr. Kim, a middle age Korean 5'10" clean shaven and dressed in a Brooks Brother suit. Mr. Kim is a former military captain of the Korean Special Forces; he works out daily and teaches Pryce the arts when he has time or not working on a special project for him. Only it all depends on what you call work, in scarecrow mind cleaning the store and stocking the shelves is just part of the job. Killing in his spare time like he was trained to do is another aspect of his job and hell since the pay for killing is better than what he is paid for working in the store why quit.

He walks over to Mr. Kim; they smile like old friends who have not seen each other in years.

"Hey Mr. Kim how is the family?"

"Fine and yours, the wife and my son say that you have forgotten them"

"Well hope you told them, that her American son will never forget her or his brother. Now what brings you to this side of town?"

Well was in the hood as you say," that brought a hearty laugh from both. But really come let's talk, as they are about to get in the car Indio walks to the car

"No it's cool, go on without me got some biz to handle with him"

He gets in the car and close the door, but just as he does Vinnie and Sal come out the pizza shop and watch the chink and scarecrow get in the car. This enraged Vinnie even more because not only does he not like scarecrow but also he hates chinks with more of a passion, only his hatred comes from the fact that his father died in Vietnam when a chink ran into his father bunker and detonated a grenade that killed his father and two others that were guarding ammunition. Vinnie turns to Sal,

"You see this shit, the chink and the nigger so the chinks are putting the nigger up to this shit"

"Calm yourself that is not going to happen, look Vin you just hate niggers I do not and the word is he is not to be touched simple" Sal says it matter of factly.

"Fucking nigger lover," Vinnie says as he gets in the car. Before Sal does Chris and Bob, call him to their car

"Hey Sal come here for a sec!"

"Yes what's going on?"

We just talked to Pryce; he gave his word, now my question is who told Tom he was going to do that?"

Chris speaks up, "look, I just met the person he seems like a straight shooter, and the loyalty is not a smoke screen. Bottom line, have no idea how or what makes him loyal to the family but he can be trusted and will put my life on that it's not him but he sure knows someone is about to do it and put the word out without coming out saying it himself or revealing the person"

"So what should we do?"

Bobby responds, while still looking at the car Pryce just got into.

"We go to the store and wait on the fucking thieves and kill them, then send Pryce the reward money"

Chris says, "He will not take the money besides he does not need it," at that, they all smile. Sal agrees that they will go to the store and wait on the thief, and as they get in the car, Sal notices the Korean hand Pryce an envelope. One thing for sure Chris was correct, Pryce does not need the money the chinks pay him well as their hit man. Nothing goes unknown by the mob; they are at a loss as to who could be behind all this. Even members of the Korean mob have no idea who Kim hit man is, if they knew it was the young kid around Mr. Kim all the time they still would not believe, but Pryce and his boss felt since no one will believe it they let it go. What they do know is he is effective, and has not failed in his mission yet. Only thing nobody can figure out is how was he able to carry out a hit when the person was on Rikers Island and he is far too young to go to Rikers.

"I know we are not supposed to talk about how you do your job, but as an old man sometimes curiosity gets the best of me, how were you able to carry out the hit on Rikers you are not old enough to go?" Kim looks at him not really expecting an answer, but hoping he would answer.

"So you mean my teacher is doubting his skills or the skills of one he has taught, you may think I didn't pick-up certain things but I did believe you me I did."

At that Kim smiles," so must tell you this is priority the person is due to testify in court Monday morning and is heavily guarded"

The look Pryce just gave Kim is one as if this will not be a problem, and now he must rearrange his schedule to deal with this. As he gets set to leave the car, Kim grabs him by the shoulder, the wife is having dinner Sunday 4pm see you then August is waiting on you. This was more of an order than a request that did not come from Mr. Kim but his wife and son. Mr. Kim knows that Pryce has never refused the request of his wife and son, the consequences for both will not be nice. The last time they missed a dinner invitation, Kim and Pryce had to scrub the entire house while she inspected and then cook for forty guests. .

"If you do you will be cleaning the house alone"

This would be a piece of cake, but Charles had a mansion in the Hampton Long Island with 12 rooms and six bathrooms, living room, dining room, and a entertainment room as well as library, the look on Pryce face made Kim realize that is the last thing he wants to be doing.

"See you at four, old friend give my brothers and mom my love" as he gets out the car he looks in the direction of Bobby and Sal and gives them, a sign that they recognized all was well.

Before the car starts, "Vinnie asks are you sure you want to place your life in the hands of a nigger?" the comeback from Sal jolted Vinnie "DAM! Right would you be willing to bet your life on me being correct?" This question made Vinnie take so long to answer that Sal had to pry the answer out of him," so what's it going to be, your life if me John, Bobby, and Chris are correct, or ours if we are wrong four against one so what's it going to be or you that fucking racist the nigger got you scared"

"Not afraid of no dam nigger, you fucking four on, let's get the fuck out of here and will enjoy watching you see the nigger suffer and then will enjoy killing you four dummies"

Sal is smiling because he is going to let Pryce kill him, he would love to see whom it is Pryce is going to lick. Nevertheless, no matter what as long as it is not the family he does not care.

Scarecrow, is walking to the club and as he passes the Chinese restaurant between Linden and autumn avenue, he notices that Dolly waited on him as he approaches he shakes his head.

"What you shaking your head for?" Just trying to figure out why you not at the club waiting on me, scarecrow ask matter of factly," is this to be expected all the time from you or is this just something for the day?" why is it a problem? Dolly asks with hands on her hips that look like Picasso painted them on her as all of her body is so finely portioned nothing is out of place.

"No just trying to figure out why you still around, look I have a busy schedule this week and we will not be able to spend a lot of time together, are you kool with that?" Pryce ask holding her chin with the tip of his finger tip, "yeah, long as you fit me in the schedule" as she moves closer Pryce has the shirt he just brought open just slightly, so she can put both her hands inside and caress his body sensually, moving her hands over his entire body. Moving her hands across his body like a blind man groping the dark, trying to find her way she lays her head on his shoulder and breathes in deeply the sweet smell of his Egyptian oil on his body and squeezes him tightly, let Pryce know she is hooked. On this day the name scarecrow no longer exists, the only ones who will know this name are those he grew up.

Not because he is about to lose his virginity, Marisol and Joan took care of that what was actually a rape. The details are still clear in his mind; sitting on the couch and having both Joan and Marisol handcuff him and then cut all his clothes off with a straight razor and no protest, well if you call singing the song "Let's Get It On" by Marvin Gaye as a protest.

But the name scarecrow represented a quite little boy in the projects, he was no longer in the projects but living in a two-family Brownstone house, where you had to take your trash outside and put in garbage cans all the houses have in front of the house or behind the wrought iron gates. He goes from elevators that do not work incinerators to dump trash or the smell of the ocean in the distance behind the projects. No this is an entirely different smell, of fresh baked bread or cakes made in the local bakeries and pizza shops smell of pizza coming out the oven. Even the nationalities of the people around him are not the same, but this kid from red hook projects has made the transition as if he has lived in this place all his life. His family is surprised, especially when his mother took them to see the new house the first words out his mouth is "Mom where all the black people?" which made the owner nervous, and his mother embarrassed.

As he walks down the street with Dolly, the wind blowing ever so lightly that his shirt gets caught in the wind showing off his youthful physique to all the women watching as they both strut down the ave like the they've been crowned the King and Queen of City-Line. This is not one of those typical New York summers that where it is so hot the devil would try to find a fan, no this is one of those days of summer in New York. The cool summer air gives this city a fresh smell of life as the day goes on, it is so cool that normally the kids would open fire hydrants but on this day, no one is bothering to open them. Nevertheless, city-line is different; these kids do not open fire hydrants. They go to the beach or the pool, which in this area of Brooklyn they do not have neighborhood pools. In and around the projects, within a few blocks of the projects you have a pool and Red Hook was no different the Red hook pool was right behind the projects on Lorraine street. Yeah to Pryce those were the good old days, now scarecrow has changed his name, dress, speech, and walk. As they make their way to the block they both see all eyes are on them, and realize from this day on all eyes will be on them and even Elizabeth Indio woman is on the block. These two are like Gumby and formerly known as scarecrow Pryce, childhood friends and families well known to each other. When they get to the corner of Pitkin and Sheridan avenue, Elizabeth is so happy for her that she runs up and kisses her on the cheek, without even saying hello the first thing out her mouth is

"You better treat her right negro" all Pryce could do is smile and turn to Indio, "How you doing Liz I'm Fine glad to see you too"

" I sorry, listen I know you think I do not like you but, when it comes to her if you hurt her you will really feel my wrath" Pryce leans back slightly, "now what makes you think I feel that way about you, could it be that you feel since I came around Indio and I have been spending time that normally you two would spend together, look Liz do not believe in short term relationships, and again I give you and Indio all the space and time you two deserve. Hell why you think when something goes on he do not find out until the next day when he is with you, listen to me she straight. She going to be more spoiled than you"

At that Liz sucks her teeth" no way she going to be more spoiled than me"

"Watch and see, we good now Liz huh"

"yeah" she says with a smile "now let's go inside and the four of us eat know you hungry she hungry and so are me and Indio" Pryce sticks out his arm as if they were together, and she grabs his arm as they smile and walk towards Indio and Dolly. "You trying to steal my guy Liz" at that Elizabeth smiles "no I have mines, and now you have yours" They go inside and Liz and the other girls go in the kitchen to fix the food, as Indio Jerry, Pryce and Gumby go in the living-room of Liz apartment to sit down and talk. "So Gumby, you ok now or you still got questions?" Pryce ask his friend Gumby shakes his head up and down," really just one" Gumby says and "what is that my friend?"

"Do I need to call you Pryce or scarecrow?", before Pryce could say anything Jerry, answers " now have no idea what you was calling him in the pjs but now his name is not scarecrow but Pryce".

Dolly heard that" I kind of like the name scarecrow" "so do I?" Liz says. They put the food and drinks down in front of them, and go in the kitchen that Pryce thinks is part of the Puerto Rican custom for women not to sit around while men are in the room together talking.

Jerry and Indio see that Gumby is relaxed in these surrounding which is because of Pryce, meanwhile Gumby and Pryce have the look of two friends who have not seen each other for years and catching upon old times reminiscing of the old days and their childhood follies. Jerry and Indio are enjoying, all the stories of the stupid things Pryce did when he was in the projects, from the rock fights, football in the snow on concrete. The only break came when Liz voice could be heard saying "where you going" when they all looked up Dolly was coming in the living-room and went and sat on Pryce lap and leaned her head on his shoulder. Apparently,

Dolly was breaking protocol by doing this but when Liz and everyone saw she was not about to leave they left her alone and Liz just joined the party and did the same thing she did.

Pryce seeing how comfortable she was, had no objections just welcomed her with open arms in fact the glow in his eyes that Gumby saw was his friend enjoying the company from him and her. In fact Gumby has not seen this look in his friends eyes since the last time the New York Yankees went to the World Series and his uncle got tickets for them to go, his friend now has that same look, even more Gumby is as always right there to enjoy the moment with him.

As if Jerry, Indio did not already know it, Gumby lets them know just how loyal Pryce is by letting them know that before Pryce left the hood he always told Gumby that no matter what happen in his life if he made it big he will be right there by his side to enjoy it with him.

After that, the look on everyone face said it all. It even changed Liz idea about him, and Dolly got so comfortable she fell asleep. In Dolly mind, she knew she had someone who was not going to abuse her or cheat on her, and was not going to let him out of her sights. Reminiscing of the good old days was good but it was time for Pryce to go, when he woke her up, she grabbed him around the neck. "What is it?" Dolly asked him" I got to go will be back later, ok you going to stay at Liz until I come back or go home?" Pryce has his arms around her 'No I will be here with Indio and Liz. What time you coming back?" she asked in a voice of a person just waking from a good nap.

"About 11 or 12," "ok "Dolly says "will be waiting on you," He tells Gumby and jerry to go get the car, when they leave out Indio, gives him a small nylon gym bag which Pryce does not inspect and heads out the door after giving Dolly a passionate kiss on the lips while gently caressing her butt. She massages his chest, like a professional only it gave him an erection. Like none other, in fact the way Pryce was massaging her gave her an orgasm that made her shake as if she had the chills.

Outside Jerry as usual is driving and Gumby is in the passenger seat, Pryce jumps in the back seat of the Z-28 Camaro Black with sparkling silver rims that even in the dark shined like the sun was out. "Where too Pryce Jerry asks, we going to Jamaica Heights, Jerry drives down Sheridan avenue until he hits Crescent street, they have time to kill so Jerry is giving Gumby a tour of the hood, pointing out the areas who controls what, All the 411 he needs to know about since he will be kin the hood. They pass by the Dirty Ones Club house, which has Motor cycles outside lined up, and a few members outside smoking and drinking. Jerry and Pryce promise Gumby, when they come back they will stop by so he can meet them all.

Jerry makes a right on Atlantic avenue, heading down this way is a straight shot to Jamaica Heights and the only two talking is Jerry and Gumby. Pryce is deep in is thoughts of his entire day, he thinks that Vinnie really has his mind set on killing him, and the only people standing in his way is Mr. John, Bobby, and Sal. It is not in his nature to rat on anyone, but his life is on the line for someone who wants him dead more than Vinnie.

The Hardy boys, who are the other gang in the hood, live on the other side of city-line and close to his Junior high school, which is in Hardy boy territory. Because the school is in their hood, they control everything, girls, money, and even an occasional school security officer. When Manuel 6'1 170lb Puerto Rican, muscular builds and star linebacker for the Lane Knights. Pryce a 5'11" 110 pound beats the second in command of a rival gang, fought in school Manny lost he lost rank, and the only way he could get it back is to kill Pryce. Pryce quickly had to learn that to win a fight in this hood not only took rank, but gains status and that the gang would then obtain status, the gang that lost must now wage war against Pryce and his family; only in this gang war, the stakes are different. This gang war between the ENY Dynasty and the Hardy boys, real problem is the ENY Dynasty has only 12 people to fight 126 of the Hardy Boys. there have already been two attempts on Pryce and Indio life already, word on the street they won't make it to prison they will be dead before police get them, and others feel that if you survive two assassinations you will survive this fight. The hood is quickly recognizing that Indio and Pryce are the two luckiest teenagers in the hood, and that these men will survive this war. This is how Indio and Pryce forged their bond, one week before this Indio saved Pryce when two Hardy boys were about to jump on Pryce and Indio helped and in one on one match, Pryce won against Manny. The fight is set to begin in three weeks, and have to come up with $300 thousand

When Pryce found out that Indio was planning to hit the Genovese crime family, Pryce convinced Indio to call it off, allowing Indio to see that robbing The Genovese crime family would create another problem they do not need. What they needed in cash to buy weapons, to Pryce that was small change to a kid who gets $250k for every hit and a bank account totaling one million dollars. Indio is nervous over the fact they still do not have the type of weapons they need to fight with Hardy Boys, Indio and the ENY Dynasty have no idea that Pryce has acquired enough guns, ammunition, and explosives to take on a small army.

This is one of the things that Indio has grown to love about Pryce, always there for him and the crew. Indio without hesitation called it off, the only thing Indio was worried about is how Pryce was going to come up with enough guns, ammunition, and explosives. Despite his insistence for him not to worry, it did because they only had enough guns and ammo to last for no more than three days and if another attempt was made on their lives again it would deplete there resources, so far they have been lucky and no serious injuries or death has taken place on their side. They cannot say the same for the Hardy Boys, who are feeling the effects of this war and everyone on the street, is already betting these unorganized little kids will win.

Which has only made the war between these two more deadly, when Pryce left the look Indio gave him was not one of fear but worry that Elizabeth and Dolly will not survive the week. Two attempts made on Indio mother, brother, and his sister killed. Leaves Indio worried, when Pryce left the guns he has in the bag are all they have and without these, t Indio does not intend to be a sitting duck without a fight. Pryce has heard rumor, the Hardy Boys have changed the rules. It surprised him Indio knew nothing about it, so Pryce despite his reluctance he called in Mr. Kim and even though, his boss wanted to help this was something he knew they had to do for their selves without help. Mr. Kim understood but Pryce knowing him, it was not possible especially since Pryce was involved only the father was not coming but the son.

After the job is completed, they must ride to china town, and meet August to pick-up the ammo. Even though Pryce wanted to pay for the supplies, Mr. Kim told him it was gift from his family to his, all he wants to know is what surprise.

The ride to Jamaica Estates, took only 45 minutes and they are in front of a store with a liquor store next to it. All of the other clothing stores, and shoe stores are closed or just about closing. The target is just up the block, he is the states star witness against the Korean mafia, if he makes it to the Grand Jury, the entire Korean mafia will take a tremendous hit.

When the Korean families, wanted the job done they all had their own hit men but Charles convinced them that he had someone who would do the job. For the York County Prosecutor to obtain a conviction on the Korean Mafia will be a huge, political boost and with elections three months away, Anthony Brown has been campaigning hard and vowed to put a dent in the mafia in his county. Out of all the organizations he chose, he chose the Koreans and the York county District Attorney's office has been seeking to obtain evidence on the Koreans for six years, now they have an insider who can give them names, dates, and all the information they need to disrupt this organization. Mr. Brown has extensive security around their informant, but none of the other families knew how to get at the informant. Charles Kim assured the families As Pryce walks down the street, that he had the man or boy for the job and besides as Mr. Kim so eloquently explained to the families no one would suspect a Kidd to kill informants for the mafia especially for Koreans who he nor can anyone link him to them.

Just like clockwork according to the Intel, that Charles gave him. The informant will come out every night at 8pm and walk for thirty minutes but he will not go past the two police cars stationed in the area one in front is blue/white further down is a brown crown Vic with two detectives also watching around the clock. He is early and the informant is not out yet, so he walks down the street towards the unmarked car and sees one in the passenger seat smoking a cigarette the other sleeping. The one thing Pryce did not do was smoke to him that was a disgusting smell, but the plain-clothes detective did not know this and when Pryce came to the passenger side, pulls out a cigarette and begins looking for a light and walks to the car

"Hey buddy can I get a light from you"

When he pushes the car lighter in so he could give him a light, Pryce has removed the 44 magnum with silencer from under his Yankee shirt and before the detective knew what was going on Pryce fired off two rounds that was muted by the music in the car and silencer, splattering blood and brains all over the car. Death came instantly for these two police officer, two down three to go was the thought in Pryce mind. As he walks back toward the, blue/white city police, car the informant is coming out the door, by the time he reaches the police car. He sees Pryce coming in the direction of the two uniformed officers, but he does not see the two 44 auto mags behind his back. As he quickly approaches the vehicle, Pryce quickly squeezes off two rounds splattering the brains of the officer sitting in the driver seat, and when the other officer and informant realize what is going on it is too late Pryce squeezed off two quick rounds into the head of the informant and police officer. The Negro Gatos [the black cat] moved like one as he reached the bushes surrounding the house with speed, he had to obtain all tapes of the confession from this informant. Just as he suspected, two plain-clothes detectives come out the house, the third was probably inside eating or watching T.V. As soon as he was, sure, both were on the porch, he came from around the bushes like a ghost and the only words the two detectives could get out their mouths

"Where the fuck you come from" and that was all the two dead in the doorway said. Inside he moved through the house looking for the tapes, he draw closer to an open door that is slightly cracked and two men are inside talking. The mirror shows a reflection of the top prosecutor from Manhattan," shit" he exclaims to himself, he hates to kill government officials because it brings to much heat but the only way to get the tapes is to kill him so be it.

Pryce pushes open the door; they thought it was one of the other officers. When the kid with the ski mask walked through the door and fires two rounds in the chest of the detective, and then turns his weapons of destruction on the prosecutor. "Look this is over, find another career" Pryce grabs the tapes and the video recording tapes, "oh the machine was on if you didn't know" Pryce never gives him a chance to respond he walks out the door. Both Jerry and Gumby smiled when they saw Pryce come around the corner and Gumby gets out the car and pulls the seat back so his friend could get in. At the car, Gumby treats him as if he was truly a mafia don, "worried for a moment, boss?" Gumby tells him. "Yeah, now you know what I do"

"No I don't"

As he gets in the car, "home or you got more work" Jerry asks, "China town take your time in fact you guys hungry?" Pryce tells them to stop at the first burger or chicken joint so they could eat. But Gumby suggest," Hey look since we going to Chinatown why not wait until we get there to eat? Got a taste for Chinese food anyway"

"Starting to like this guy more and more" Jerry excitedly explains. Why you did not think of it? Pryce asked Jerry,

"A partner that helps out, besides you need two people one man cannot handle you and since he knows how to deal with you, we got a game plan for you"

With WBLS playing music, Frankie Crocker is the night DJ who plays the old soft music that is only good if you in the bedroom with a bunch of naked females, which he remembers a date with two freaky dikes who are going to come looking for him in about one hour. If he is not at their house, but they will understand and they know he never misses a time to roll in the bed with two females at the same time. Something most kids only dream of, but at his young age he is enjoying the time and this is the only thing that brings him any relief from the strain of the up-coming war.

They pull up in front of the restaurant, Jerry has brought Pryce here many times, and the only difference now is only this time instead of waiting in the car he gets to go inside the restaurant. To him it seems odd that Pryce will walk into the restaurant and go straight to the back with no interference, he has seen him do this on many occasions. The place is full on this Saturday night and smells, of egg rolls and other dishes that are being prepared. There is only one table for two people, Jerry and Gumby take the seats. Pryce walks towards the back, on the left is the office and as he knock a Korean cracks the door slightly to see who it is and when he recognizes that it is Pryce he lets him come and searches him. The search is not finished because Mr. Kim tells him "no need he never carries a gun into my place of business, besides his brother is eagerly waiting to see him"

"Now before you and my son take care of your business, we need to know how the distribution of the heroin will be done.'

. Please explain to these gentlemen, but first let me introduce them to you" Mr. Kim exclaims. But Pryce stops him, "no need had no idea they would be present at this meeting, and really have no need to know who or what they are in my line of work it is better for me"

Pryce spoke as a man in control, and the men around the table were impressed at the way this kid was handling the meeting and how he handle the job. Even the guards at the door were indistinctly nodding there approval of him, as Pryce explains how he has centers set to distribute the heroin and cocaine throughout the city and how he has targeted certain areas and how some will be off limits to avoid wars with other families.

One of the old men at the table who looks like he is sixty years old, Pryce figured him too be the Don of all Dons as he spoke Pryce could tell that his observation was correct, what came next was even more of a shock.

"We know that your friends are getting ready for a war, and in need of shall we say some firepower, so I am ordering all of our families to ensure that you have anything you need to be victorious, even manpower if you need"

At that Pryce was about to protest, but the old man held up his hand as to silence Pryce, and the old man spoke again

"Mr. Kim tells us you are a proud man; he also says the rules are no other family can get involved. We not as far as you know and know about two attempts on your life as well as your Don, we have a lot invested in you and we want to protect our investment" Pryce on the inside is excited, as the old man continues. "

So by the time you get back three trucks will follow you, unload the items you need safely and take care a few of the Hardy Boys,"

Even though he pronounced it, wrong Pryce knew he was referring to the Hardy Boys, the meeting ended with Pryce paying for the food, as they walked out the door. Mr. Kim told him" August would be in the office in a minute, in the mean time our security will bring your friends to join you in a meal with my son and a few of his friends"

Pryce remains seated on the chair he was in when the meeting was going on, and when he looks up August grabs his arm and they begin wrestling on the floor. While the others stand around and watch, Jerry and Gumby walk into the office and are introduced to August and the others. They take the same seats left vacant after Mr. Kim and his associates leave.

So let us get down to business, we have only a few minutes to eat and get this stuff back to the other side of the city. August smiles, just like you to take care of business before eating, remember wars on an empty stomach. Pryce interrupts him, "yes but our friends are without weapons, that is my concern" August and the other shake their head at the approval of a man who is more concerned with his people than he is his own well-being.

Listen "worry not we have people watching them until you return and have every since you left the hood as you say"

Jerry and Gumby have shocked looks on their faces, "so you have been following us?" Jerry asks

"No we were watching your friends and the last word we have is all is well, Indio is outside now with a few of your friends now"

Gumby looks at Pryce, "well glad you on our side" at that they all laugh and August and the others see the relief on Pryce face when he was given the news of Indio and every one. The good meal came with good company and old stories. As the night moved on, so did they as they began their ride back to Brooklyn. Pryce and August are in the car with Jerry, Gumby, and Pryce in the back seat. Behind them are three moving trucks loaded with everything they need, and behind and in front of them are guards armed with M-16 rifles submachine guns, and grenades.

Indio looks at the clock in the Television shop window and sees that its going on 1 and Pryce and them are not back yet, Angel tries to comfort him "Hey negro got nine lives, he coming back in fact I feel him coming down that block in two minutes"

Indio tries to laugh, but Angel knows he is worried and so is he but trying to keep a good face. "Amazing how, in such a short time we cling to a man we hardly know Indio" as they are talking Willie sees three moving trucks coming in their direction with what looks like Pryce car, as he ask "Yo is that Pryce car?" Indio sees the car, "negro Gatos" which means black cat brings a smile to his face.

Because no other cars are on the street, one-truck parks in front of the Television repair shop, the other in front of the liquor store, and the other pulls up along side of the club.

When they see them, Pryce quickly issues orders "get everyone out the club and get these trucks unloaded" Angel goes in and pulls everyone out the club, while Indio is talking to him Marisol and Joan are at the club waiting and when they see what is going on they go up to him and whisper

"you good Negro we know why you missed, we got you though what you need us to do?" Joan asked him, with that Pryce says, "Just help unload the trucks" August is across the street talking to one of the men, they had watching Indio and them, and Indio lets Pryce know about the car and after he tells him what they were doing. Indio lets out a sigh of relief, "so you're watching me now?' He puts hands on both his shoulders

"Yes someone has too, and you would the same for me now let's go unload the trucks" Indio grabs his arm, "no you've done enough tonight someone is inside waiting on you, go we got this,

Go," he says in a demanding voice. Pryce says his good bye to August and tells him he will see him tomorrow, as he goes inside Dolly is sitting on the couch with a long dress shirt on with just panties on under the shirt and wrapped in a blanket. He kisses her on the cheek, "so that's all I get," she says to him. They passionately kiss, as he begins to caress her body only to find that she has no bra on and the spot between her legs is wet. "Starting without me huh?" as she begins to undress him he picks her up and then stops, "Yo get dressed we going to my crib ok" she does not even protest, moves quickly into the next room and all she did was put on a pair of shorts and sneakers that look like a size one.

Outside, they have just finished unloading the second truck and now working on the third, as Pryce and Dolly walk out. "Yo look I am going to my crib" Pryce lets Indio know where he is going

"No you not, not without security" at that Frankie is smiling. Both Jerry and Gumby look like kids on Christmas, with the new toys. Indio looks at him and tells him "go we will finish this, in about twenty minutes." the entire time they had people watching for any signs of the Hardy boys spying on them, all is clear and just as they finish unloading the trucks the Koreans bring to Hardy boys around the block tied and gagged. Indio looks at them, and tell the Koreans "you know what to do with them" they are hauled off; whatever they do to them is fine with Indio. He is just glad they are on his side not the other, as the countdown to the war has grown shorter.

Jerry is walking behind Pryce and Dolly, Gumby is across the street looking as if he was not with them. You would think the Hardy Boys would have figured this out, but they fall for it each time and this time was no different. A car comes racing down the street, Jerry and Gumby already on point because that is the only time cars come down this block is either the cops are chasing them at that speed or this is a hit and since no police sirens could be heard they knew something was not right. The guns ready and cocked, the car tosses a grenade out the window and it lands in front of Dolly and Pryce as he grabs Dolly and jumps behind a car the grenade goes off. Jerry and Gumby fire on the car and the other join the shooting. The car careens into the back of the moving truck, with bullets all over it as Indio races up the street to see what is going on with Pryce. The fire is so intense that Indio cannot get near the fire and neither Jerry or Gumby, as they watch the fire they have not seen that Pryce and Dolly have escaped the fire. They head to Pryce house quickly, as she grabs one of his guns

"Don't worry I know how to use this she points to the gun, so if we die we going together"

At that Pryce did not even protest all he did was grab her hand and they headed, towards Linden Plaza knowing this was going to be a fight the Hardy Boys did not want, and it just dawned on him if they knew or thought it was going to be this hard. At one point, he was curious as to why they just did not just blow up their houses but that would violate the rules of the game. Hell Pryce thought after this and the fact they changed the rules, it is time for him to change the rules a little bit and he thought hell fuck it.

"Dolly you want to get some revenge?" Pryce ask her

"Dam Right but when and how all we got is one gun between the both of us"

"Come on" he tells her as they continue walking down the street, this side of the street like most of the streets in this city the street lights are only bright enough to light one side of the street while the side they are on is cloaked in darkness. Pryce cool dark complexion is perfect to hide as they move through the darkness, so just as they moved during the explosion they have disappeared into the night without anyone seeing them. While everyone thinks they are dead what better way to strike, and if Dolly can use a gun like she says she could the Hardy Boys are in for a real surprise and he is about to find out just how good she is.

Indio, Gumby, and Jerry are standing in the middle of the street screaming Pryce name.

PRYCE!

The fire department has arrived, and put the fire out and two bodies are in the fire. Because they are charred, all they could say is that it was a man a

Chapter 10:

Hardy Street Massacre

Its 12mid-night and Pryce is on edge after the explosion that just went off, but he had his woman with him and he now had to make sure they both survived this. As they walk to the projects called Linden Plaza, he stops by a pay phone and calls the cabstand. When they answer it, the voice on the other end is excited to hear his voice but nobody is in the stand, they are out looking at the explosion.

"Look baby face do not tell anyone you heard from me, And in fact you need to come get me"

"But" she is cut off and told not to ask questions just do as she is told

"Ok give me five minutes, I'm going on break just hold on are you packing"

"No we need some heat"

'We who are you with?"

"I and Dolly are together"

"Make it two leaving out now" she grabs her car keys and heads out the door. The other driver sees her leave as he tells him to watch the stand she will be back in an hour or two."

Baby face is 6'0" long black hair that touches her buttocks and curves better than the streets of any city, she has the hots for Pryce and she also has the hots for Dolly but she is not into women. From where they are, it only takes no time for her to reach them and the way she is driving anyone could do it in two seconds. As she pulls up, they are talking to some men and when Pryce sees them, he cuts the conversation short.

"Hey baby face you quick"

"Look just get in and where we going"

"Empire Blvd turn around and" before he says anything she responds

"Look I drive cabs I know my way around the city, just give me the address"

1124 Empire Blvd"

Dolly is enjoying the ride, snuggled with Pryce in the back seat, she has no idea where he is going and just does not care as long as she is with Pryce it does not matter. Uncle Willie got Pryce the apartment, and this is the first time in eight months since his uncle got the apartment for him that he has used it. The light traffic only shortens the trip, and Dolly surprisingly has fallen asleep if only briefly it was a power nap she desperately needed so does Pryce, but he has no time for naps or sleep he will do that another time not now. As they stop in front of the building, the apartment is between two brownstones on each side and a garage for each brownstone. Baby face and Dolly notice six cars with tinted windows are sitting in front of the apartment they tell baby face to leave, and as she takes off Pryce and Body greet each other and head quickly into the house."Well what is going on?"

"First what is it going to cost me for them?" Pryce asks Body with serious tone in his voice.

One of the people who was standing behind Body introduces himself.

"My name is Lunatic, body has told me about you and guess tonight we will see how good you really are but the price is 4million" Pryce goes in the back and grabs two duffle bags, and brings them back into the living room. Dolly saw him come and take the bags out into the living room, and knew that they contained either drugs or money. "So where the does the lady fit into all this?" Lunatic asks Pryce.

"She is my driver, and the four of us will ride in one car together. Oh, by the way fellas nobody is to live we will do a three-house sweep.

Rhino is Irish and about 35 or 40 years old and ask the question no one else thought about, "Why are we using silencers I like noise"

"I want this to be a surprise when they find the bodies it will be a mystery as to who did this"

"So you want us to get in and out without creating a scene?" Rhino says matter of factly

"Now you get the idea."

'I like to kill silently it allows you to come and go as if nothing is wrong so when do we leave?"

"Now" as Dolly comes out the room fully dressed in body armor and two nines strapped to her sides. She walks and puts her arms around his waist and in a soft seductive voice asks Pryce.

"Are you ready to go" and leans on his chest the smell of his oil is gone but the love she felt in the car is not. The hired killers in the house are looking at them and wonder how long these two have been together and for him to take her with them she must be good not only in the bed but in the streets.

"Sorry to interrupt you two love birds but we have work to do or was the money for free," Lunatic says looking at them

"Well lets go, we are ready" as they head out the door. The streets are desolate especially for a city that prides itself on the fact that the city never sleeps, well this side of the city is definitely sleep. For this neighborhood, most of the families living in this area work and have kids Pryce age that attend school regularly. However, so does Pryce when he is not killing people, and he hopes that when this is all over him and Dolly will have time to be with one another.

On Sheridan Avenue Indio and Mario are standing on the corner talking, while all the rest are on the other end talking among them. Indio is trying to explain to Mario that they need to have peace between them; the war is not something they wanted or need between each other. Jealousy comes from Pryce quick name recognition, he like all others in the hood surprised by the fact this black kid who just moved into the hood is, respected, disliked.

One thing for sure and the expression on his face shows approval, despite it being short lived. The new kid came through for them, now they are on the block-mourning one of their fallen soldiers. Mario admits to no one but himself that he is amazed, and wishes they could have gotten to know each other despite making them walk naked through Prospect Park.

"Yo B what is the name of the crew" Indio pauses for a few minutes

"Let's just say welcome to the East New York Dynasty"

On this day, the new crew formed a name that Indio and Pryce if he was still alive would appreciate. However, the main thing is, the ENY Dynasty now had to earn its respect and place in the hood, and from the looks of things, this latest hit by the Hardy Boys put a damper on this.

By now the news has spread that Pryce is dead and so is Dolly, the Hardy Boys with this move let the hood know they finally got Pryce so now Manny would regain his position. With Pryce death the Hardy Boys sent three messengers, to add insult to injury but the insult only flamed the anger of Jerry and Gumby who expressed their dislike by killing two of them and dumping their bodies in the big green dumpster used by the clothing store Rondell's to dump their trash.

The one they left alive, Gumby makes strip and walk back to his hood naked with the message lose one you lose twenty-one. Indio was not upset and nor did he try to prevent the death of these messengers, even when Jerry and Gumby went to apologize Indio wanted nothing of the kind and helped put the bodies in the dumpster. The only thing Indio did say was when he asked Gumby, about the butt naked move.

"Gumby what's with the butt naked move?"

"Oh something we do in the projects, when you get guys coming from outside the hood you make them walk back home Naked At that they all laugh, and Jerry is the first to ask

"How many guys Pryce did that too?"

You really want to know"

However, on the other side of town, little did they know people were about to die. Hardy Street is about to become a street full of bodies, the level of violence they are about to experience is nothing they have ever seen before, when Tony returns Butt naked and embarrassed he will quickly forget all about that and focus on what will be the most devastating level of destruction only the mafia is capable of doing.

Dolly is driving and Pryce is enjoying the ride as the passenger, Lunatic and Body in the back wondering if their insurance policies are paid. At no time did they think they would be killed by one of their own in a car, they figured a gunfight would end their lives and if someone else does not drive it will surely be their last gunfight.

"Hey look slow down you were doing 120, you going to kill us before we get to the place."

As she slows down, they turn down the street past White Castle restaurant and have one block to go before they reach the Hardy Boys corner block. Pryce directs her to ride pass them, nobody on the corner seems to pay attention to the passenger as they come closer. Pryce could see them all in front of the store, and he tells dolly to go back around to where they came from and as he is about to get out the car she grabs his arm.

"Where are you going without me?"

"Look just keep the car running in fact; turn the car around the other way."

"Hell no we going to ride past them just so they could see our faces."

As he is about to get out the car he looks at her, "what" she exclaims, he shakes his head and gets out the car. She is willing to die with him, they have not had sex and she is willing to die for him, what better person to have as your bodyguard Pryce fell in love instantly. Instead of whispering to himself so only he could hear it, he said it loud enough for her to hear and since he was close to the car she taps on the window and with her lips let him know

"I heard that" at that he moves on towards his mark.

Up the block, two people are sitting on the steps and before they could say, anything Pryce lets off two quick shots from his 44 auto-mag with silencer and they fall just as quickly as they got up with a single shot to their heads. As Pryce, Lunatic and Body are on the steps of the house and the others are in position, the three men open the door that was open. Two men sitting on the couch watching television and others are in the back. Body motions for Lunatic to go upstairs, a little kid comes running up the stairs from the basement and the mother is right behind him. Before the kid or his mother knew what was going on Body puts two 357 mag into the child and mother. Quickly, they move through the house and when they come out nothing is alive. They walk down the steps Dolly opens the door "Get in" she tells him, as the door swings open they jump in as if nothing is wrong and so does the other cars.

"I'm not going to be saving your black ass all the time" she looks at him and smiles

"I love you too" Pryce looks at the road in front of him and the destruction behind him, and the woman next to him without a show of emotion for her to read Pryce is happy Dolly's on his side,. She snaps him out of his world, "Hey where we going?"

Still going fast, Dolly turns on Atlantic Avenue. As they come to the house, Body and Lunatic drop them off without anyone seeing them enter the house. Dolly goes to the kitchen and gets

Pryce a glass of juice out the fridge, and when she comes back in Pryce is laying on the couch with his feet on the floor.

"Here you go" hands him the drink and as he takes it, he looks at her. Dolly is just wearing her bra and pants. Pryce looks at the way her body is shaped and now is the time for him to make his move, he grabs her by the waist and pulls her to him and as she does. She breathes heavily and he could feel her breath on his face, he begins to slowly caress her back and kiss her lips ever so sensually.

She takes off his shirt, and she admires his muscular form from his work out with body and August. He picks her up and takes her to the bedroom, as he lays her on the bed, they begin kissing, Pryce puts his face between her legs, and she moans

"oh Pryce eat papi eat it like its cake" he continues until she reaches her climax and she then goes down on him and he looks at her sucking on him like it was a tootsie roll pop and she wanted to see how many licks it takes to get to the center.

"Oh ma dam that good keep going, oh yes"

The sex was good and Pryce and Dolly are in each other's arms until the doorbell rings, Pryce goes to the door. The only person that knows he is here is Body, and when he looks in the peephole, he sees Body.

"Why are you here so early, in fact why are you here?"

"The Kim's want to see you for breakfast and sent me to make sure you come"

"Come in before the neighbors see you" they come in and Pryce offers him something to drink.

"No, we must get going"

"Sounds urgent, what is going on?"

"Well he knows about the killing, it's all over the news"

Pryce was too busy enjoying the company of Dolly, and when he turns on the T.V Dolly walks into the living room and the news is talking about the deadliest massacre the city has seen in years, the New York Headhunter serial killings was nothing compared to this and they have no witnesses.

"Good Morning Peter the police say the family after returning from a night on the town found their family dead, and as they went for help they fund more bodies laying inside the local club, and other outside the apartment building. What they police found as they continued their search for witnesses was more death and in each house, no survivors could be found." The news reporter is a short white woman with black hair shoulder length, as she is talking they see Tony standing in the background. His entire family was killed and he looks like a man who lost his own life, the others standing around are crying over the lost of friends and family.

"They dead, they killed them and dumped their bodies in the trash dumpster and made me walk back naked" "Yo what happen here, who did this?"

We thought you could tell us", Yo them niggas D.B.L." the letters simply mean down by law and was a status given to those who show the type of bravado in the streets as they have done the title is only bestowed on a select few and the ENY Dynasty quickly obtained this status.

"How many are dead?" Tony asks this question while looking at all the police, and emergency crews.

"They stop counting after they reached thirty no survivors Tony, we was hoping you could tell us who did this

The tone of Victor voice was desperation in hopes that this fight would stop tonight, he knew Tony must find out who is capable of this amount of destruction. Victor knows Indio and Pryce, he once was their best friend in school until Pryce, Manny got into it, and even now when they have a message, they send him. All the others they sent come back naked; one has to look at what they have done now and imagine what they did to deserve this.

Tony grabs Victor by the shoulder, "Yo go get everybody and come to my basement in five minutes, need to get dressed and tell them I said now" as Victor quickly takes off Tony goes inside his house to get dressed.

"So where are we going now" Dolly ask Pryce as she sits on his lap and puts her arm around him.

"We are not going anywhere you are going home and I am going to have breakfast with my boss" she stares at him quizzically

"No I am going with you, and besides you are supposed to meet my family today"

"I am but after I finish with this meeting, then I will be at your house at 4pm for dinner"

"Why so late?"

"I have another meeting to attend after this I was hoping we could stay together until later but something has come up."

She snuggles up to him "I want to be with you where ever you go, you going to meet another woman tell me just don't lie to me"

"I am not lying to you, look come here" he grabs her by the hand and takes her into the bedroom. He sits her on the bed.

"Look we are not going to do this, I want to be with you and I do not believe in short term relationships, and cheating is out the question, just do as I ask and will see you later ok"

She sucks her teeth "Yeah " she has tears in her eyes as he goes into the bathroom to shower, she comes into the bathroom and sees him through the shower curtain naked and undresses to gets in . They make love in the shower, as Body is in the living room watching T.V. they have come out the shower and as they dry off.

Pryce goes to his closet, and picks out his tailor made suit compliments of Mr. Kim and his tailor the smoke grey Calvin Klein suit, white Yves Saint Laurent Shirt grey and white tie and black oxfords. She sees this

"You not going to no meeting you going to meet some bitch"

"I am not will you chill out please"

CHAPTER 11:

THE MEETING

Inside looking out the window, at the fire down the block and they have sent Joan and Marisol to gather information.

A'ight this is the beginning and we need to be on top so get ready we are about to hit them hard" when he says this someone knocks on the door Marisol comes in wide open.

"Yo b you got a phone call Its Pryce" they all get excited and Indio is the first out the door followed by Gumby and Jerry. Once they get inside Indio grabs the phone,

"Hello, yo b what is going on we thought you were dead yo how is Dolly?"

"She is fine and at home, waiting on me to come for dinner look gather everyone will be back in the city in an hour be at the house nobody is to be late."

"Ok I got but what is going on we ready to hit them now"

"No look at the news for once you will find out a lot if you watch news."

"Glad you alive but wish they would kill your attitude" they all laugh at that. Gumby and Jerry are glad to see Indio smile, hell nobody was until the phone call came through as Gumby thinks to himself so is he. .

The police are outside investigating the carnage; this is the first incident the police had to investigate tonight and the only question that remains is who and what caused this. Police are talking to the residents about whom and what they saw and the police confused by the lack of cooperation by the residents. In this neighborhood police expect the residents to tell them everything, and when these residents do not it leaves the police with one question who and what has the residents so afraid they will not tell the police what has taken place.

Detective Flannigan a 40-year-old descendant of Irish parents and a veteran of the NYPD for 23 years, and tour commander for the 75th precinct 11-7am shift, at 5'9" even at his age the daily wok out in the gym allows him to maintain his physical appearance.

As he approaches them " Lou what you got for me?", Lou is the abbreviated term for lieutenant, and Lt Abrams is in charge of the detective homicide division and just like

Flannigan a veteran of the NYPD Lt Abrams is taller than Flannigan at 6'1" 200 lbs is a New York Jewish native of Brooklyn Williamsburg section. "6 DOA's and 5 seriously wounded who might not make it"

"Kind of like the incident on Linden Boulevard, are we any closer to finding out if these two are related to one another?"

"Afraid not Flan, nobody is talking see no evil hear no evil and speak no evil"

"Look Headquarters is already breathing down my neck because the Mayor is breathing down theirs so we need to work on this and make some arrest" anytime the city is gripped by violence of this magnitude, the police make a lot of fictitious arrest and while the Hardy Boys are just gathering together. Tony is well aware of the possibility that the police will be coming around to get him and a lot of others, because this time the city on edge because the police have no idea who to arrest and what charges to arrest them for, so the police in this area need sacrificial lambs.

Tony and has everyone inside his basement, the police are still on the street questioning residents and retrieving bodies that are scattered all over the place. The meeting has just begun and has heated up, some are upset at the destruction and the death toll from someone, and some are upset that some want to end this war to avoid any more death. Everyone knows that Tony is in charge now and as he quiets them down what he says send shock waves through the entire room.

"Look we need to make peace with the kids until we find out who did this, we have lost too many of our people for this to continue and we are going to align ourselves with them"

Hector is the first to speak out

"Why are you doing this?" With those words the entire room is quiet, and Victor speaks up "are you serious, really do you not see what has been done to our neighborhood, how many more must die before we end this war? Somebody brought a level of violence to us, either it's the mob or one of enemies and until we find out we must stop all wars even with the kids"

"So Manny rep means nothing?"

"Maybe someone should tell you that he is dead and so will we if we do not find out who did this"

"So!" Hector exclaims as if this level of violence is the norm for this neighborhood, and even through his protest Tony sees that really he is just making a bunch of noise because he really wants this to end just as bad as he does but putting on a good front. Nevertheless, the looks and the sounds of frustration and desperation for something to be done, to end it was more or less the real tone of these men voices. No matter how much they hated to admit it they really wanted this to end because they have never experienced this level of violence, that they were exposed too o other gang has in all the years they have been operating.. Moreover, there can be no coming back from this, the only noble and safe thing to do was surrender and pray for peace. This is exactly what Tony had in mind when he brought them together, he was going to send victor to talk with Indio and Pryce. Victor was the only one of the Hardy Boys Indio and Pryce trusted and liked, in fact, he used to hang out with them until Pryce and Indio began fighting with the Hardy Boys, then the friendship ended just as quickly as it began. However, whenever they had messages to send they would send Victor and he would come back safely, so now he does the same only this time it is to establish a meeting with them and call a truce. The idea brought relief to those in the room, while some expressed unrest over the decision they were glad it was ending. They are really in shock at what these unorganized kids have done to them and on their turf.

The news of the destruction has made all the major news networks, and the mob is even more surprised. The problem is the only one they know is Pryce and has no idea how to deliver the message. This news has shocked the entire city, the level of destruction has the city declaring a mob war, but the only problem is that they had nothing to do with the mob. Therefore, the question had the city police stumped with, no answer s and everything quiet the policed hope that this will die down and not escalate any further.

What surprised them next was the visit they would get from Victor. Indio quickly told him that the meeting must take place tonight, they will not wait until the next day, or any other day it ends now was the strong words Indio relayed to Victor. As Victor heads out the door, he turns and asks them

"I am sorry we had to end our friendship because of the fight between your friend and Manny, but It's nothing personal just business"?" at that Pryce stands up and walks to him looking him straight in the eye without flinching and says

"How do you separate the two, you was willing to kill us but now you're trying to protect your own lives" but I feel no pity for you or the dead. See you knew we were at a disadvantage, no guns no experience bad combo for the streets especially in this town. You gave us no help and no pity; man you lucky I do not kill you for putting us through this. No in fact, be at the diner under the Crescent street station in one hour we walking out with you and will wait no more than 40 minutes for you to come back after it is on you.

"Marking my next take over" at that he walks off, and Indio bewildered by what his friend has just told him. Those thoughts are on hold for now, as they move along the city street in silence with Victor in front of them and home court behind them. Well really, ENY dynasty has home court advantage after the massacre Pryce left; he was now targeting the mob. Little did they know he was casing their operation from the inside? The reason he chose this area and place, every Sunday the mob has all the daily proceeds from the weekly races, and numbers funneled through this restaurant. According to Pryce resources, 4 million dollars and he wanted a piece of the pie. He was trying to devise a way for them to do so, while he at time hates to admit it he likes Jerry for better or for worse he likes him. Even now, he says that he can figure out how to hit the joint and come off without them knowing they were there. He let his security team do the work now he had Gumby, how could he go wrong. Pryce knows that lady luck does not shine always now is the time to seize upon the moment because when bad times hit and they will, all hell going to break loose and those standing around now will no longer be around.

As Pryce and Body enter the driveway beautifully manicured, a garage that holds six cars and Pryce car is sitting in the driveway washed by the hired help. As always, August has already come out to greet him and as they exchange pleasantries, his father comes to the door.

"Well you have been busy, last night but glad you came nonetheless"

"Yes lets go inside and talk" they walk inside and Ms.kim is coming out the kitchen to meet him

"My son you come to breakfast we now have to call you come every Sunday from now on, or else"

"Yes mom" is all Pryce could say as they head towards the dining room that is set with the morning meal. Maia is black woman thirty-five –forty years old, and a recovering alcoholic, who always makes Pryce his favorite French toast with sausage.

"Well It's about time the food is about to get cold next time you be on time or else"

"Why you are two ladies threatening me this early, all I want is to eat and talk with my boss"

"Mr. Kim is not the boss Ms.Kim is" Maia says matter of factly

They sit down to eat and Pryce is sitting next to Mr. Kim, when his wife leaves the conversation gets serious.

"So tell us about last night is it over or will you still have problems?" Mr. Kim asks mildly

"All I can say is we brought some time to get established, they have no clue that we did this and we are not on anyone's radar"

"Is it possible they could retaliate, or are they licking their wounds as you say?"

'Well licking their wounds is more like it now, we are going to begin operation in the next twenty-four hours heroin, cocaine, marijuana etc., all the sites are set and the people."

"How will you distribute the heroin if you do not have people to do so?"

"Yes good question, I have three distribution areas in Brooklyn that are ready to go well really nine the other five belong to my uncles"

"I am aware of your uncle's distribution, and the others are receptive of such a Youngman running the operation?"

"Not exactly" Mr. Kim has a puzzled look on his face, but Pryce quickly responds to the look

"Let me explain, they have no idea I run the operation all they have been seeing is men make the drops and pick up"

"I see" Body and August listen and with showing are smiling at the fact how well Pryce dispelled any doubts about his ability to handle the drug game like a professional. The breakfast continues with Pryce eating 12 pieces of French toast, along with small talk from the men that focused on the future of his organization and the assistance that he would receive from the China Town families. Really filled him physically and mentally, as him and Body knew that one day they would have to b urn that entire block down. His only concern is why Pryce did not do it last night and chose to wait, something he had to ask.

"Let me ask a question, nobody has asked?"

"What is that Body?"

"Why did you not kill everyone we had silencers, so nobody knows we did this just want to know why?"

"Good question and my best answer is this, to buy time and knew they would look at that amount of destruction and flinch. Look all I want is for us to get off the ground, this helped and they will not bother us for two years then we will get rid of all of them the same way."

"But if they do we will not seek your permission to kill the entire neighborhood"

"Fair enough but have one question well really a problem" they look at him and he continues

"Well I am listening"

"Who is Luis Martinez, well what kind of person is he. I want a piece of his action on the lower east side, but do not want war." The mention of his name raised Charles eyebrows that let everyone in the room know he was something to consider but what he tells them only emboldens them to be more aggressive.

"Ok if that is what you want then know this will bring to much heat from all sides the police and his family, so what is so important about this operation?"

"The lower east side brings in anywhere between 3 to 9 mil, that transforms into a twenty mill for us if we have his distribution which stretches into the Bronx." All of them are shaking their heads in agreement, for how Pryce is thinking, but nobody told Pryce that the families in china town have already tried this and failed. As Mr. Martinez said, he will only do business with his people.

August is sitting next to his father, who agrees with Pryce this brought time especially for what Pryce is planning, none of them but August knows that Pryce is really planning a war with people he will never know or see.

As he prepares to leave Body offers to drive him back, but he grabs the keys for the Lincoln Continental puts on his shades and drives off.

"Make sure nothing happens to him, if they scratch him you scratch them" was the orders Kim's gave to body and he was glad to hear those words. The ones who scratch him will not live to see another day, his favorite student and despite the Kim's claim to him Pryce was Body son he had lost and now found.

The ride back into the city will take an hour, as he looks at the clock that reads 1pm; he only has an hour when he gets into the city to meet with his uncles. He sent Julio on a mission to collect from the heroin spots in Busch wick, Crown Heights, the Busch wick area is already playing with the cheddar, and Julio had green light to do what is necessary to send a message. After they talked, Julio said he had to be home for dinner tonight that his sister was bringing a new man around to meet the family, and he would see him after dinner at the club.

Years ago a man walked into a police safe housed and killed his informant, and eight police officers, and disappeared into the night. After former Assistant District Attorney, now Deputy District Attorney in charge of Organized crime is looking at a violent war that everyone claims is a mob war. This same man who life was spared by the killer all the city is looking for who killed 6 police officers guarding a state witness who is also dead, but headed not the warning of the killer and chose instead to pursue this mystery man. Only one-question remains who is the mystery man that killed a state witness and six officers guarding him. For now, this mystery man will have to wait, ordered by his boss to investigate further and report to no one but him on this mob violence. Everyone will find it too late, and this allows the ENY dynasty the breathing room it needs to gain strength. So just as the building went up in ashes tonight so will any leads on who did this, since the truce that is about to be called on the other side of the city will seal the fate of these young warriors.

Now all they know is that it took place on Genovese territory, and the ones dead have no ties to the family. Which begs the question of why are they dead and not unless this is the Genovese, fighting local gangs for power. Dumb thought for such a prominent prosecutor whom one day has the potential to be the head prosecutor for his county, And if he could solve this he would surely be a candidate for the seat. Solving this is like finding out who shot Kennedy; he needed some inside help and knew where to get it. He lives in the hood where all this took place and Mario owes him a favor so it was time to cash in. As he waits on the elevator Regina Maris is 5'10" long jet black hair and thick in all the bright places, and the heads turn in the office when she move smoothly through the office but the only one she has not been able to catch is Anthony Brown. The both of them are waiting on the elevator, and even though he can smell her perfume and see her standing beside him, he is attentive on the task ahead that is finding out who is behind this gang war.

The word is that while Maris is a hard nose prosecutor like him, they say that the only way she gets a confession is by having sex with her defendants.

"Well well another hot case or just another case of you being shot in the ass."

"As usual, why are you in so late trying to get someone to touch your tummy with the taste of nuts and honey?"

As the elevator door opens, he gets in, looking back at her, he sees the indignation in her face at the comment he just made, but before the doors close, she responds

"For a homosexual you have served more people than McDonalds, your Golden Arches have been real busy"

The door closes and they both disappear behind the door. All the insults made him realize that Sterling Parker the Paralegal Manager have not been together in over three weeks, and wonders what he is doing now and just as the doors open he thought it was his floor but it was actually the floor his lover works on. Fate would have it that just as he was thinking about him, that he would end up getting on the elevator with him and both of their eyes lock on each other.

Sterling is more athletic than Anthony is; Sterling was a star football player until he started chasing a different type of footballs. Two years older than him, both began their careers at the Queens DA's office three weeks apart. During one of Anthony trials Sterling was in charge of keeping the notebook, and the first day they met these two have wanted each other more than hogs want slop. In the homophobic work place culture, these two have managed to keep their love life relatively quiet, despite the rumors no one has concrete proof they are lovers and so women in the office doubt Anthony is gay and have went so far as to trap him off in his office and strip like they was in a strip bar. No one really cares, especially not the top brass that he is gay, all they want is results, and when they give him a job, he completes it. He is their most reliable prosecutor in the office, and touts a 96% conviction rate that is including the fact all of his convictions come from trials not guilty pleas.

Anthony does not believe in plea bargains, so defense attorneys prepare for trial and will not bother with negotiating pleas. Sterling on the other hand, despite his sexual preferences, the other paralegals like him and he can rally the troops when it requires.

"Well hello stranger, sad that you live with your lover and he is a stranger"

"You know my job creates these situations, it is not the first, and it will not be the last"

"It will not be the last for who you, for me it is. No way will I live with my lover and the only time I see him is when I come to work, so if you cannot make time for me then you have two weeks to get out"

Anthony is shocked at his response "Really you cannot be serious" he looks at Sterling face and sees that it was no joke.

"Ok look let's talk about this when I get back home"

"No the conversation is over get out ASAP, find another lover, little advice if you going to be a hoe at least get paid for it" the elevator doors open and he goes in one direction and Anthony goes in the other towards their cars. That is the second person tonight that has called him a hoe, nobody was supposed to know that he was in a three some two nights in a row. Anyway, that will not stop him from getting to Mario.

As the ENY Dynasty, waits inside the diner with early morning customers. Indio and Pryce wait at a table that seats four. Jerry and Gumby are casing the joint, they see the money, and who is who. While the money is rolling in, so does Tony and the crew. Jerry and Gumby quickly stop them and search them, but Pryce stops them

"No need they will bring guns into this place, not if they want peace.

"Look let's get down to business"

"Certainly" Indio tells them to have a seat. They sit with Pryce, Hector, Tony, and Indio.

Tony begins by apologizing to them, but Pryce quickly stops him

"Look no time for the sad stories, you did what you did. Now the question is how we end this" the tone in Pryce voice made it clear that complete and total surrender was all he was thinking and accepting.

Tony asks "Why are you being so nasty towards us we are willing to end this you should be happy"

Indio in not so nice terms tells him

"Look Tony, you made us grow-up we went from childhood to manhood in 0-60seconds well in two days we went from child to man, the Hardy Boys altered our nature, so let's stop the foolishness like you are not to blame for this."

"Ok let's talk; here is what we suggest full control of the Hardy Boy turf and 60% of all money made" Hector responds so loud that the customers turn and look at him

"Are you fuckin crazy, no let's just end the war without money or you getting anything other than peace"

"No, we could keep this war going" Indio grabs his arm and whispers in his ear, and then he speaks

"We want 60/40split on all action; we will give you a safe passage and help increase your distribution by 40% with our routes. There will be no more war between us, the first time any of your people violate this we will be back to burn this neighborhood down" when Indio stops speaking Pryce says something, as he leans his elbows on the table.

"Back in the 1800's or1900's look up the Chicago Fire, the whole city burned down. This will be New York fire, only your neighborhood will burn down women, and children will die for your people stupidity."

At that, Pryce and Tony are face to face. Tony had to admit, being in the room with these two made one fear the worse if the answer was no and then again it was no time to show weakness or fear. The war was over and now he had to lead his people, building the crew was one thing but rebuilding lives is something different.

All the people came to this neighborhood, country for a better life; now these families lost fathers, sons, uncles, nephews, and women casualties that was intentional. The ENY Dynasty has made it easier for them to move on with their plans, only the next move will set the city on fire and leave a trail of bodies more than the wars fought by this country.

How do you defend against something you cannot see or know anything about? Pryce says if they have not found the New York Headhunter, the serial killer that gripped the city with fear who they seem to think he is dead but who knows maybe he just got smarter the East New York Dynasty has.

THE END

www.ingramcontent.com/pod-product-compliance
Ingram Content Group UK Ltd.
Pitfield, Milton Keynes, MK11 3LW, UK
UKHW041936190726
13854UKWH00004B/1625

9 781365 481826